The Trouble with
JEREMY CHANCE

ALSO BY GEORGE HARRAR

Not As Crazy As I Seem

Parents Wanted

The Spinning Man

First Tiger

Radical Robots

*Signs of the Apes, Songs of
the Whales* (WITH LINDA HARRAR)

The Trouble with JEREMY CHANCE

George Harrar

Illustrations by Elizabeth Thayer

MILKWEED
EDITIONS

© 2003, Text by George Harrar
© 2003, Cover and interior art by Elizabeth Thayer
All rights reserved. Except for brief quotations in critical articles or reviews, no part of this book may be reproduced in any manner without prior written permission from the publisher: Milkweed Editions, 1011 Washington Avenue South, Suite 300, Minneapolis, Minnesota 55415.
(800) 520-6455 / www.milkweed.org / www.worldashome.org

Published 2003 by Milkweed Editions
Printed in Canada
Cover and interior design by Christian Fünfhausen
Cover and interior illustrations by Elizabeth Thayer
The text of this book is set in Century.
03 04 05 06 07   5 4 3 2 1
First Edition

Portions of the chapters "Explosion" and "Hero" first appeared in *Cricket* magazine, January 1999.

Special underwriting support for this book was made possible by a gift from the James R. Thorpe Foundation.

Milkweed Editions, a nonprofit publisher, gratefully acknowledges support from the Bush Foundation; Emilie and Henry Buchwald; John Cowles III and Page Knudsen Cowles; Dougherty Family Foundation; Joe B. Foster Family Foundation; Furthermore, a program of the J. M. Kaplan Fund; General Mills Foundation; Jerome Foundation; Dorothy Kaplan Light; Marshall Field's Project Imagine with support from the Target Foundation; McKnight Foundation; Minnesota State Arts Board through an appropriation by the Minnesota State Legislature; Navarre Corporation; National Endowment for the Arts; Debbie Reynolds; St. Paul Companies, Inc.; Ellen and Sheldon Sturgis; Surdna Foundation; Target Foundation; Gertrude Sexton Thompson Charitable Trust; James R. Thorpe Foundation; Toro Foundation; United Arts Fund of COMPAS; and Xcel Energy Foundation.

Library of Congress Cataloging-in-Publication Data

Harrar, George, 1949–
    The trouble with Jeremy Chance / George Harrar.—1st ed.
        p.   cm.
    Summary: In 1919, following a disagreement with his father and his first whipping by a belt, twelve-year-old Jeremy hops a train to Boston to meet his older brother, a soldier returning from World War I.
    ISBN 1-57131-647-7 (cloth : alk. paper)—ISBN 1-57131-646-9 (pbk. :alk. paper)
    [1. Fathers and sons—Fiction.   2. Country life—New Hampshire—Fiction.   3. Coming of age—Fiction.   4. World War, 1914–1918—Fiction.
5. New Hampshire—History—20th century—Fiction.]   I. Title.
    PZ7.H2346Tr 2003
    [Fic]—dc21
                                                                                2003000529

To Mom and Dad

The Trouble with
JEREMY CHANCE

The Trouble with
JEREMY CHANCE

CALAMITIES

JANUARY 1, 1919, wasn't much different than any
other day that lighted up our hillside above Derry, New
Hampshire.

I woke with the first chickadee pecking at the seed I
left on the ledge outside my window. My nose was almost
froze shut, like the snout of an ox left out in the cold too
long. Bite was curled over my toes, and he didn't even stir
when I pulled my feet out from under him. I never saw a
dog sleep so deep. I raised up a little and stared at his eye-
balls; they were fluttering under the lids. I'd bet my 1906
silver half-dollar he was dreaming of chasing rabbits
come spring.

Some folks looked for New Year's Day to turn life
quick for the better, as if pulling December off the calen-
dar meant good times would suddenly roll up to your
door. Not me. I'd learned enough from seeing twelve new
years come and go to know the world wasn't going to
change a stitch.

One of those things that never changed was my pa

mounting the stairs by twos just after dawn. If he got to me before I was up, he'd shuck off the covers and give me a cold-air bath for lying in late. Sometimes he'd put his big icy hands on my neck, and I'd just about jump out of my skin. So lickety-split I hopped out of bed in my union suit and waved at Pa as he came around the doorway. He grunted at me as a good morning, then moved on down the hall. I think he missed the fun of colding me.

I took a minute to scratch under my arms and down my back as far as I could reach. Wearing the same long red underwear all winter caused some powerful itching. Done with the scratching, I thumbed off my spruce gum from the headboard of the four-poster. It felt hard as a stone to my tongue and took some delicate chewing to get soft again. I was awful careful 'cause you could lose an eyetooth chomping on it.

Gum was the fortification I needed to set about my first chore of the day: cleaning out the chamber pots. That was one job I wouldn't have minded leaving behind with the old year. We had an outhouse twenty yards back by the cedars, but none of us went out there in the middle of the night, especially in winter. My morning chore was to pull each pot from under the beds and run them out to Nellie, which is what my ma named the outhouse. She thought it more polite to say you had to visit Nellie than that you were going to do your business at the outhouse. My pa never called it Nellie. He'd just kind of thumb out back and head for the door. We got the idea.

Gathering and dumping the chamber pots was a job

best done fast, without a lot of thinking about it. So I ran into my pa's room and got his pot and then into Cousin Sadie's room and got hers. With both hands occupied, I went carefully down the stairs and out the back door. The snow was almost two feet deep, and walking down the path Pa'd cleared was like going through a cold, white tunnel. I emptied the pots as fast as I could and ran back to the house. Nellie wasn't any place to linger.

My next chore was to light the Acme Six Holer. I'd taken special care the night before to fix a fine bed of pine branches topped with ash logs so the fire would draw fast. I had that old stove heated up in minutes.

Then I strengthened myself on some of Cousin Sadie's Indian meal porridge. She always put it out first thing and then went back upstairs to fix herself up for the day. I hurried eating the cold porridge so neither she nor Pa would come down and find more work for me. Today I'd set aside for deer hunting, and I lit out for it just as soon as I was through scraping the bottom of my bowl.

It's no boast saying I invented a special way of hunting that was a whole lot easier on me and the deer. What I did was leave my rifle at home. Pa didn't understand how a person could go hunting without toting a .30-30 Winchester. I figured that by hunting my way the deer didn't end up dead and I didn't end up dead tired carrying nine pounds of steel and wood over my shoulder.

When deer sense you ain't fancying to kill them they don't mind at all you watching in on their habits. I hiked a mile into the woods beyond Wesley's Dry Goods where most real hunters are too plain lazy to walk. I plowed through knee-deep snow in some places, which was a considerable hindrance to getting anywhere fast. But not being so old as to have to work all day, I could spend as much time as I wanted slogging along and not mind a bit. Pa said twelve was a fine age to be as long as you did your chores and didn't get into trouble that required a whipping. He made a lot of sense.

Shakers' Hill rewarded my effort. It was a small mountain where this religious group called the Shakers went to get close to the Lord. They'd meet up there and pray for hours. When they felt the Lord come inside them they did a sort of dance that looked like shaking. Pa said the Shakers believed in a simple life of hard work and not having children. I didn't mind working hard sometimes, but I couldn't see making a religion out of it. As for children, it was kind of hard being against what you were.

I came up here to pray sometimes, too, but I never did any shaking. I guess that's because we're Congregationalists. When Ma died last fall I climbed up to say good-bye to her because I figured it was the closest place around Derry to heaven. A year before that, when Davey joined The War, I came here to ask He Who Made Us to please bring my brother home again with all of his arms and legs.

I didn't always go to Shakers' Hill to ask for things. Sometimes I went just to talk a bit. There wasn't a better place to get God's ear to yourself. If your eyes were keen enough you could see clear to the Atlantic Ocean. Davey used to say you could see forever from up there, but I never did. Maybe his eyes are better than mine.

The Shakers never came up here in the winter, so I knew it would just be me on the hill, and maybe some deer. Just as I got there I saw a herd of seven whitetails parading ahead of me. A couple of the smaller ones stopped to nibble off the lowest branches of the birches and oaks, which were planted in rows by the Shakers about fifty years ago. The bigger deer stretched their necks to reach the higher branches. Every once in a while they turned around to listen.

I was thinking how nice it would be living free outside like a deer, with no chores to do and nobody telling you when to go to bed and when to get up. Then I spotted this one old doe who was so skinny I could see her ribs. She looked too weak to even lift her head to eat. I could tell she wouldn't last the winter, which was always about two times longer in New Hampshire than most other places. It made me wish I'd brought some bread and cheese for her—and maybe for myself, too. But Pa said feeding weak deer was sticking your fingers into nature's business. He said that starving was nature's way of thinning out the population of deer or people so the stronger ones would be carrying on the species. I saw plenty of both going hungry around Derry, and even if it was the way things were supposed to work, it wasn't a pretty sight.

I knelt there watching the deer for a while until my leggins started drawing up water from the snow. I jiggled about some to shake the cold from my legs, and that frighted the deer a little. They bunched together and looked around. Then they did something strange: they moved away right past me! I sat still as a log as they came about ten yards from my right shoulder, paying me no mind. I guess I was downwind from them and they couldn't smell me. The weak doe came last, and she was limping. "Keep going, you can do it," I whispered so as not to spook her. She stopped and looked over and sniffed a little, probably hoping I was something easy to eat. I guess I disappointed her by being alive. Then she looked at me with a wondering look, as if asking why I was lying there in the snow. After a few seconds she hobbled on to catch up with the other deer.

I followed their tracks for a bit and got to puzzling. Here were deer half again heavier than me tiptoeing through the snow. But ninety pounds of me had a powerful struggle to step through it. It didn't seem logical. Or fair.

I was thinking I'd ask Pa about this, but I knew he'd just say I was better off figuring things out for myself. He didn't like all my questions, and I had a million of them. For example, one morning I knocked my cup of coffee on the floor, and Pa said I was all thumbs. As I was cleaning it up I wondered out loud to him, "If God is all powerful, can he make things fall *up* instead of *down* if he wants to?" Pa shook his head like I was asking something foolish. Then he said everything he knew that was worth knowing about the world he had figured out for himself, and that's the way it should be with his boys. Well, it seemed to me I'd be better off knowing the right answer from him rather than thinking up the wrong answer on my own. But I didn't dare say that. Anyway, I figured God *could* make things fall up if he had a mind to, but then they'd always have to fall up, or else people would think he'd made a screwy world.

I walked home trying to figure out all the tracks I was seeing. In one place there was a thin line in the snow, like a field mouse makes, and then the line stopped just as if the little creature had disappeared. An owl or hawk had probably swooped down and lifted it off somewhere to be supper. In another spot there were partridge feathers lying all about, but no partridge. Some animal like a fox must have caught it.

By the time I sighted smoke drawing from the chimney of our house, I was soaked through to my skin from pushing through the snow. The cold had snuck inside my wool coat and was freezing the flesh off me. Such days with high blue sky were the worst for hiking. The sun made a body sweat like a horse, and then the wind colded up icicles under your shirt. It was time to get inside and fortify myself with cinnamon coffee.

I broke out of the woods on the east side of our cabin, which was built of cedar logs by Grandpa Chance about eighty years ago. Truthfully speaking, he did a sorry job. Even Pa says that. The upstairs leaked rain on my head in a heavy storm. The north wind whipped through the living room during a blow. More critters made home in our walls than in the woods.

Now it's a strange situation when your house is falling

apart and the man inside is a fixer of things by trade. Pa repaired things for people, but he barely lifted a hand for our own place. He said it was no use trying to work a miracle. He said God's hand itself would have a maddening time making our cabin fit for comfort.

Well, when the ceiling timbers got around to falling, I didn't want to be sleeping underneath them. Nor did Cousin Sadie. She and I had the same fears, and we told them to Pa. He looked at us like we were being childish, but I saw him laugh a little under his mustache, like when he's hiding something from us. Then he out and promised as how he was saving toward building us a better place. He just needed a few good months of work. And with The War over now, Davey would be coming home soon to lend a hand.

When I got to thinking about some things, like a new house, I forgot other things. Like Licker, our neighbor Cutter's old mare that we boarded in our barn. She was twice as big as most anything else that came onto our land and could kick up a bucketful of noise. But I was thinking so hard on a new house that I didn't have a notion this fool horse was pounding around the woodpile dead aim on me. There was nothing to do but get run over, which I did.

Lucky thing Licker recognized me right off as the boy who combed her hide smoother than a pig's shank now that Mr. Cutter wasn't up to doing it. She leaped me like a purebred jumper, just scraping my forehead with her hind legs. I wasn't hurt much at all.

But there came Cousin Sadie, pulling up her skirts and

galloping from the front door. She scooped me up like I was a flatcake stuck to a skillet. She said, "Jeremy Theopoulos Chance, don't you ever get out of the way of things?"

I hated when she used my middle name like that. How could any two parents who weren't crazy between the ears name their boy Theopoulos, even in the middle? It's not like we had any Greek blood in us. Pa just heard the name one time and said he liked the sound of it.

"I do get out of the way of things," I said to Sadie. "Spent most of the morning fine as could be in nobody's way."

She looked me over tip to toe, then set me down on the snow. "I don't deny you have your calm moments. But see, setting your pants afire yesterday, now that silly horse running you down today. You got to spread your commotions out like other folks do. Else you be in for a mighty short time on earth."

I didn't see how I had much choice when Licker or other such calamities appeared in my life. Seemed the Lord was in charge of them goings-on. As for the fire ashes that Pa threw onto the snowbank yesterday, anybody might have sat on them unawares.

Pa said trouble had the curious habit of passing right by other folks to dance with me. Well, I'm proud to say I made it twelve years without more than my little toe shot off. To be truthful, stepping out with trouble was a darned sight more interesting than sitting all day on your backside, even if it did get burned now and again.

Sadie gripped my shoulders in her big hands, which were strong from pulling cotton last season. Then she shook me out like an old rug. Shaking was her cure for most anything that befell a body. She could shake the ticks off a dog's ear, no effort at all.

"I'll just be hollerin' for your pa," Sadie said when she let go of me. She took a deep breath, which meant the whole woods was about to get an earful. I covered my ears with my hands—still my head rung like the inside of the steeple on top of Central Congregational.

"JaaaaMes Chhhaannce, . . . Come HoohME!"

You have to understand that Sadie weren't like other folks who lived in these parts. She was Pa's cousin, and she'd just come from the South three months back after Ma died. Pa said I needed a woman around the house to look after me, and we were lucky to get Sadie, who didn't have a family of her own. What we didn't know was that she'd be bringing hollerin' with her.

To hear Sadie tell it, yelling was as natural as talking down in Boone, North Carolina, where she was raised. People called to each other up and down the mountains like we did from one room to another. She swore that the Appalachians was one place in this world where Mr. Bell's invention would never catch on. She didn't put much stock in such a contraption as a telephone. People would soon lose knowing how to use their voice boxes, she liked to say.

Sadie had nothing to fear on that account.

"CoMMMe HooHME, Jaaaames!"

Bite started yapping from behind the barn and then took off into the woods. That hound dog could howl up a racket his own self, mostly in the dead of night when the moon was turning full. But he wanted no parts of Sadie's hollerin'. Fact is, there wasn't a creature in the woods that didn't wish to be buried down under when Sadie took to the airwaves. Except Licker, that is. That horse was deafer than an anvil and, truthfully, not much smarter.

"Hoo-ooOME, James," boomed Sadie again as loud as any bomb. The sound just about split open my ears.

"Sadie, don't holler no more, please," I said and tugged at her skirt. But she just swatted my hand away and cupped her hands around her mouth, belting out as loud as she pleased.

"I ain't hurt, Cousin Sadie, really I'm not," I said. "There's no need to call Pa."

Standing straight, Sadie were near tall as Davey, a head higher than any woman I'd ever seen. She had to bend over to look me eye to eye. When she did her face twitched with pain. She reached back and rubbed her hip where Licker squeezed her against the barn door the day she arrived, purely by way of making friends. "I know you're fine," she said and then dragged me off with her toward the house. "I'm calling your pa to supper. He's working over at Coventry's."

Mr. Coventry's barn door fell off last nor'easter, which is a storm that rolls up the coast and lasts for three days and blows off anything that's not nailed down. Pa was just getting around to right it because of how busy he was. People called on him to fix anything from doors to dolls and barns to bicycles. "Nothing too big, small, or newfangled" was his billing. He was specially masterful working with wood. The wagon he hitched to our horses was no more than a dozen pieces of wood and iron when Pa rounded them together. Some folks said he was as good as the Shakers at making things, and he should try his hand at chairs and such. Pa liked hearing that and always said, "I've done some pieces in my time. Maybe I'll get back to it."

Whatever he was working at, Pa didn't take to being interrupted. I knew that for sure. I told Sadie, "He don't like you calling him, unless it's some danger."

"You wash up," she said, "and let me mind your pa."

INFLUENZA

THAT FIRST NIGHT of the year 1919, a fierce wind pawed at the house like a great bear. After we had our fill eating Sadie's special New Year's meal of ham and blueberry sauce and cornbread, Pa told me to bring in extra wood 'cause it was going to be a cold one. I jumped up from the table to do it because tending fire was my favorite chore.

I had a fine blaze going by the time Sadie got done washing the dishes and plopped down in Ma's rocker. The slats on the back groaned as always, not being used to a woman as big as Sadie. She must have weighed twice as much as Ma, and I was sure one day she was going to split that rocker in pieces. I wasn't really hoping that would happen, but if it did, I sure wanted to see it.

Sadie pulled out her sewing and said she was going to put the finishing stitches on her favorite comforter that very night. She'd been saying that every evening since she came north. I think she must have been taking stitches out every morning just so she could have the pleasure of putting them back in at night.

Pa paced the cabin like he had something worrisome on his mind. Maybe he was thinking of Ma not being there with us, because she sure loved the evening fire. Or maybe he was thinking of the new house he was going to build us. Finally he stuffed his pipe with tobacco and sat in his rocker. I found myself a spot on the floor between him and Sadie and wrapped myself in Ma's afghan, the one she always pulled around herself on bitter nights like this. When I closed my eyes and felt the fire on my face, I could almost imagine it like before with Bite nuzzling my hand and Davey whittling his wood and Ma rocking beside me.

She caught The Influenza in the early fall and was gone in three days. She was walking around fine as could be one minute, baking pumpkin bread and talking about how she was going to put up double applesauce for the winter so there would be plenty for when Davey got home. Next thing we knew she was coughing and fainting and turning purple. Pa had to carry her to bed. She died before we could even get Doctor Willard out to see her. When he did come he said there wasn't anything he could have done anyway. Her lungs had filled up on her until she couldn't breathe. He said this Spanish Influenza was a mean and quick killer, and there wasn't a medicine that could stop it. More of our soldiers were dying of it than bullets. The War would surely end soon, he said, but The Influenza might not.

Doc was right. The War did end a month after Ma died, but The Influenza kept killing, though not as much. Pa said there was no way to make peace with a disease. We buried her on the back hill near the old maple. In summer the tree would spread its leaves over the grave and shade her from the heat. In the winter the bare limbs would let the sun shine through to warm her. Pa declared that spot the perfect resting place.

He built a white fence around her to keep Bite and other creatures from digging in the mound of dirt. I visited her often. Sometimes I took her things, like her knitting needles or a canning jar, and stuck them in the ground. Ma always liked to keep busy on earth, so I figured she would want to in heaven, too. I took books with me to read her, like *Call of the Wild* by Jack London. I think maybe she would have preferred the Bible better, but Pa wouldn't let me take it out of the house.

Pa and Sadie and I sat close and quiet in front of the fire till our faces turned orange and glowed as warm as the embers. Then he opened the bookcase, which he built last summer. I still wasn't to touch it, seeing as how I had this knack for knocking over things just by getting near them. I couldn't see how I could spill over a whole bookshelf unless Davey and I were fooling around, and he wasn't home from The War yet. Still, Pa said I'd be wise to stay away from it.

It was strange how I'd start out thinking of one thing, like the bookcase, and end up thinking of Davey. I couldn't imagine him fighting the Germans. I figured he might be the only one in the whole 26th Yankee Regiment to have gone through The War without using his rifle, unless he shot off in the air a couple times to make believe he was being a soldier. Davey hated the idea of killing any little thing, like a spider, let alone a big thing, like a person. If a hen stopped laying eggs for us, Pa put her on the chopping block and handed *me* the axe. I'd kill the creature quick, and he'd hang her up to bleed out. Then Ma and me had the chore of scalding the flesh to get off the pin feathers, which were the new ones that were just starting to grow. It was a terrible job to pick off every one.

I can't say I much liked turning chickens into dinner, especially the ones who followed me around the yard. I'd give them names sometimes, such as Hopper and Teddy, for Mr. Roosevelt, who Pa says was the best president we ever had. He voted for Teddy in the last election, but Mr. Wilson won. Pa doesn't like Mr. Wilson for getting us into The War when he promised he wouldn't. Pa says a man should stand by his word.

My favorite chicken was Long John, who had a bum leg like the pirate in *Treasure Island*. I read that book last year, and sometimes for no reason I started singing, "Fifteen men on the dead man's chest, Yo-ho-ho and a bottle of rum." I didn't have any idea what that meant, but I liked the words just the same.

Anyway, Pa told me I shouldn't call the chickens anything but "chicken." He said it wasn't wise giving a name to something you were planning to eat later. Turned out he was right. After I had to cut off Long John's head one night so we could have something for dinner, I stopped naming our chickens.

I would have been more use to the army than my

brother. I would have gone, too, if I could have passed for eighteen. I look older than twelve—everybody tells me that—but I have to grow some fuzz on my cheeks before I'd pass for eighteen. It's too late anyway because the Germans surrendered and The War is over. They signed the Armistice almost two months ago at exactly the eleventh hour of the eleventh day of the eleventh month, which is November. Preacher Stone said at church last week that this was the war to end all wars, so I guess I won't ever get to see what fighting is like. Pa says it's just as well.

He sat down in his rocker and opened the Bible, which was his father's Bible before him and his father's father's before that. The cover was almost worn away from so many hands touching it, and lots of pages were stuck together. It looked like a book that had gone through Noah's flood. Pa laid the big Bible over his lap and opened it to the string marking the page where he'd left off.

"Where was I, Jeremy?" he said. He always asked me that to see if I'd remembered anything from the night before.

"God was mad, Pa, and he was getting ready to punish the people."

"Punish them for what?" Sadie asked, as if she didn't know. She knew the Bible about as well as the back of her hand.

"For having other gods and sacrificing to them. God didn't like that."

"God *doesn't* like that," Sadie said.

Then Pa began reading. "Deuteronomy, chapter 32,

beginning with verse 23: I will heap mischiefs upon them; I will spend mine arrows upon them. They shall be burnt with hunger, and devoured with burning heat, and with bitter destruction: I will also send the teeth of beasts upon them, with the poison of serpents of the dust."

Pa kept reading as I poked the fire, but I didn't do it too much 'cause he said it was wasteful to burn the wood up fast. Looking at the hot red embers I imagined myself being cast in the fire and burnt because of something I'd done wrong. At least that was better than being bitten by beasts, especially poisonous serpents. Just thinking about them gave me the all-overs.

". . . I would scatter them into corners," Pa kept on reading, "I would make the remembrance of them to cease from among men. . . ."

It was bad enough to be burned up, but then to be forgotten by everyone as if you never even lived—that was horrible. Pa said our memories of Ma were something that would never leave us no matter how long we lived. For the first days after she passed away, everything I touched or did reminded me of her. When I held her afghan to my face, it was like smelling her sweater as she hugged me before bed. When I ate applesauce, I could see Ma standing at the sink peeling apples and humming to herself. When I lit a lamp I remembered how she carefully filled them with kerosene each morning. And every winter night like this, sitting in front of the fire, I could close my eyes and feel her in the room with us. Sometimes I wished I'd never have to open my eyes again.

After a while Pa's voice got slow reading the Bible, and
Sadie started dozing in the rocker. Me, I wanted to stay up
and feed the fire some more. But Pa stood up and stretched
his arms over his head saying as he always did that we
needed to rise early tomorrow to get a jump on the day.

"It's not that late," I said. "Couldn't you read some
more? How about Davey's letter?"

It had reached us in December, after the peace was
signed but before my brother had gotten our news about
Ma. I used to think how strange it was that for us she was
dead but for him she was still alive. Pa read the letter to
us so often that the paper was almost falling apart. We all
knew every sentence by heart. Still, the words sounded
new every time we heard them.

"I guess I could read it once," Pa said, "then it's
into bed."

He went to the bookshelf, took out the envelope, and
pulled the letter from inside. "Dear Ma," he read, and
as always I teared up hearing that, "and Pa and my crazy
little brother Jeremy." Little? I bet he wouldn't even recognize me when he got home. My head reaches the coat
hooks now, and I can see in the barn window without
going up on my toes.

*I guess you heard The War's over. The news
came to us one morning as we were sitting in
our trenches watching our big guns pound the
German positions about a half-mile away. Then
suddenly everything stopped, and we looked at*

each other wondering what was happening. We heard shouting and cheering. When we stuck our heads up and looked across No Man's Land, there were the Germans waving at us. We knew it could only mean one thing: The War was over! Those boys were as happy as we were to be done with it.

The worst battle I saw was at Saint-Mihiel, which is in France, in case you didn't know. Some say it turned The War and forced the Armistice. The woods were filled with barbed wire and machine-gun nests and big holes blown open from all the bombs dropped there. You never knew what you were walking into when you stepped into No Man's Land. At any moment they could be shooting mustard gas at us. You always had to have your mask ready.

I was lucky to come out of there with no more than a few bites from the nasty bluebottle flies. Then we moved on to the Argonne forest, and a bullet grazed my right shoulder. I don't mean to worry you. It was painful for a few days, but the doc patched me up and sent me back to the front line.

As bad as the fighting was, it's the afterward I hated the most. There was a field of German bodies lying half dead in front of us, and there wasn't enough medicine or doctors to keep them alive. We were supposed to walk the field and

*bayonet the bodies, "to be sure," like our
Captain Kingston says, so they didn't have a
chance to turn on us later. It was also better to
put them out of their suffering.*

*Well, I'm no good at killing, Pa. When you
took me hunting I always made a little noise to
scare the deer. You knew that, didn't you? In the
fields here I pretended to bayonet the Germans.
One boy rolled over just as I was making believe
to jab him, and he plugged me. There doesn't
seem any justice to it. I was sparing him, and
he shoots me. I guess he figured I was going to
finish him off, and he wanted to get me first.*

*So I might not be as good at ice picking or
chopping wood, least till I heal up completely.
But I'm alive as you all and itching to be home.*

*They're shipping out the wounded every
week now, and I'm on the list because my shoulder picked up an infection. It's nothing worse
than I had when I tore my leg open with the axe
a couple years back. I'm not sure when my turn
will come to leave. If I have a chance I'll send a
letter telling you, but you know the army, Pa—
they don't give you any warning of anything! If
I'm still in camp for Christmas I might be dining with none other than Woodrow Wilson. I
know he isn't your favorite, Pa, but he's coming
to visit the troops, and imagine if I got to see
the president of the United States.*

*Besides coming home early, the infection
to my arm gets me out of lice treatment today.
They make you strip naked and then spray lye
on you from the cootie machine to kill the little
critters. I don't know which is worse—the lice
in your hair or the lye in your eyes! It's like
when Ma gives us castor oil, Jeremy. The cure
is worse than the constipation.*

See you all soon. . . .

Your devoted son and brother.

Pa put the letter back in the envelope, and we all just sat there staring at the dying fire.

SPITE

THE NEXT DAY STARTED like every other in January up in these parts: bone-numbing cold. It was so bitter that when I let Bite outside to relieve himself he was scratching the door to come back inside before I sat down at the table again.

Cousin Sadie made her cornless fritters for breakfast. It seemed to me that if you didn't have something like corn to put in your fritters, you shouldn't call them by that thing. It just made a body think how much better the fritters would be with corn in them.

Pa had work to do in town at Wesley's, shoring up the storage shed roof that was sagging under all the snow we'd had this winter. "Might have to replace a beam," he said. Then he took his cup and saucer and fork and spoon to show us what he was planning. Sadie couldn't get straight whether the saucer was a wall or the floor, and we both started laughing. I told Pa that he'd need a mighty big spoon to hold up the roof. He could see there was no use trying to teach us anything and took apart his model of the dry goods store. As he did, his fork dropped to the floor, and as usual Sadie saw some meaning in it.

"A woman's going to visit," she said. "I've never seen it fail. Drop a fork, a woman comes to visit."

Pa stood up from the table, shaking his head. "You've got more notions about things than there are things," he said.

"Mark my words," Sadie said as she cleared away the dishes. "A woman's going to visit."

It happened just like she said. It was just past noon when I was sitting down at the kitchen table ready to eat the sourdough bread she'd made. Before I could get the first bite in my mouth, Pa ran into the cabin and told me to start pumping water. He dropped his coat on the floor, rolled back his sleeves, and lathered up his hands. Then he brushed his hair back from his forehead like before church and pulled on his great coat. In a second he was bolting from the cabin again, but not before telling us to stay put.

"Ain't that peculiar," Sadie said as she went to the window. I followed her, and we ducked side by side under the curtains. Sitting in the front of our house was a spit-shining green Stutz Bearcat like I'd seen in a magazine picture. A man in a gray suit stepped from behind the wheel and opened the rear door. Out from under the winter top of the automobile appeared a woman, except she didn't resemble any I'd ever seen. There was so much fur on her she looked like she was wrapped in a bear. Sadie called her a lady.

Well, this lady peered all about, especially off in the distance where the land dipped away and Derry lay below. She looked toward our house, too, and Sadie and me ducked quick, laughing a little at nearly being seen. When I raised my head up again, Pa was taking the woman's hand and helping her over to the edge of our land to look at the black walnut, of all things.

It was a grand tree, sure enough, eighty feet tall if an inch, and about thirty hands around. Davey and I measured it once by putting our hands one after the other all the way around. When the wind gusted up that tree dropped nuts like balls of hail. I liked to carry one in my mouth near all morning before getting to the meat of it.

The walnut tree was interesting all right. I'd climbed it dozens of times and fell out more than once when Davey shot stones at me with his slingshot. Still, it seemed to me that it was the Bearcat that deserved the looking up close, and I had a powerful wish to go out there.

"I don't think Pa'd mind me taking a look," I said and started for the door. Sadie's heavy hand fell on my shoulder, keeping me still. "What's going on?" I asked her.

"Your pa and some fancy lady are looking at a tree."

I knew that much already. What I meant was, what's going on beyond what I could see? Why of all things to look at in the world was this fancy woman staring at Cutter's black walnut? She touched the tree with her white gloves. Then she pulled them off and rubbed the bark with her bare fingers. After some more talking she and Pa shook hands, and the lady took again to the backseat of her automobile. The man in the gray suit cranked up the Bearcat and got inside. That beautiful machine kicked up a spray of snow as it headed out toward Possum Road.

Sadie and me pulled away from the window just as Pa came back inside. He looked mighty pleased, like I hadn't seen him since Ma died. He tossed his cap to the ceiling and yelled, "Praise the Lord, good times are coming!" He grabbed Sadie around the waist and danced little circles in the room. Then he grabbed me, too, and I laughed and stomped even though I didn't have any idea what I was happy about. But if Pa was happy, so was I.

Sadie finally broke away and smoothed down her dress. "You figuring on wedding that woman?" she demanded.

"Wedding her? Well what if I am? What if I am?"

"Then you can get someone else to do your cooking and cleaning 'cause that woman ain't lifted a finger in all her life, and I ain't staying on as some rich woman's maid."

Pa stood grinning at her. "Now I didn't speak of marrying, did I? What would a lady like that have with me?"

"That's what I want to know," Sadie said.

"It's like this," he said as he sat down at the table. "I met her this morning in town, outside the Dry Goods. She was telling old man Wesley how she's outfitting a cottage down by Hampton. Twenty-two rooms she's got and just for herself and a barrel of cats."

I let out a whistle at that. You could put together all the cabins along Possum Road and not come up with twenty-two rooms.

"She needs furniture for the whole place, and she won't take none other than black walnut. She wants a dozen chairs, a dining table, a cabinet . . . didn't even care to discuss the cost." Pa scratched his head at the craziness of it. "And where's the finest black walnut north of Pennsylvania?" I hadn't been further south than Nashua, but I knew where Pa was thinking. "Thirty paces from our door," he said, "that's where."

"But that ain't our tree."

You'd think a boy who had reached twelve years old in more or less one piece would know when to keep his mouth shut. But not if he's named Jeremy T. Chance. Pa looked at me like I'd sworn at him. I thought he was going to carry me straight to the woodshed.

"It hangs mostly on our side," he said leaning toward me, "don't it? I say, don't it?"

"Yes sir," I answered, but we both knew the walnut grew from Cutter's land, and that made it Cutter's tree.

"I'll just speak to him," Pa said as he stood up, "make him a fair offer. We're reasonable people. Been neighbors going on forever. We even board his mare for him. He'll understand this is an opportunity a man can't pass up." Pa started pacing the floor. He was talking to us, but it seemed like he was talking to himself, and neither Sadie nor I spoke up. "A man's got to make a living, and he should be working at what's in his blood. If one rich lady sees the fine job I do, the word will spread to her kind in Boston, even Newport where the Vanderbilts and Carnegies go for summers. They'll be asking for me by name . . . for us, Jack Chance and Sons, Furniture Makers. That black walnut will make us a handsome start. There's boards enough from it to fill up a couple of mansions." Pa rubbed his hands together, just itching to work with wood. "And Jeremy, you'll be learning a trade from me, make yourself a fine living."

I'd never gotten around to telling him that I was expecting to sail coal schooners down the coast when I grew up, not make chairs and such. But this didn't seem the time to let him in on my plans. I just nodded, not wanting to get between Pa and his dream.

He went off to Cutter's telling us again to stay put. I was getting awful tired of staying put, especially with so much going on outside. Sadie handed me a broom and said that sweeping would help take my mind off things. I didn't see how using my arms would keep my mind busy, but I did as she told me.

It wasn't more than a little while before Pa came tromping back in the house yelling, "Devil take him!" His fist rattled the cups on the kitchen table. "If I still had my logging boots I'd give that old man's face a case of the lumberman's smallpox."

"James Chance," Sadie said, "such a thing to say."

"Don't cross me," Pa said, whirling on her with a

fearsome look, and I decided not to ask him exactly what the lumberman's smallpox was. I figured it had something to do with the spikes on the logging boots, which were sharp enough to pock your skin if your face had the misfortune to run into them.

Pa swiped his foot toward Bite, who hightailed it to the front room. "Cutter's so old his brains have turned to water and leaked out his ears. I'll tell you, he don't make a word of sense muttering about his wife and that tree like they were one and the same thing. He should be in a place somewhere for crazy old people before he hurts himself." Pa started across the cabin, turned and came back. "He wouldn't even listen to an offer. Just rocks inside that shack of his, not a care for a neighbor who's helped him more than once. Well, I'll fix him." Pa opened the door to his tool closet and reached for his axe.

"You ain't taking an axe to Cutter, are you, Pa?"

He didn't say anything. Sadie said, "Of course he isn't." She didn't sound too sure herself, though.

He left the house without even putting his coat back on. I ran to the window to watch him head off toward Cutter's, but Sadie pulled me away and handed me the broom again.

This time Pa was gone for a long while. I heard pounding, then nothing for a few seconds, then more pounding. I imagined Pa axing his way through Cutter's door. I imagined him swinging the axe through Cutter's table and chairs and through his cabinet and bed. I imagined him breaking Cutter's windows so the snow would come in and the old man would freeze to death. Even worse, I imagined him swinging the big axe at Cutter.

I hated thinking poorly of Pa, but that's what I imagined.

———

He came back with his sleeves rolled up and his face dripping with sweat. I ran to the open door and looked over at Cutter's to see what I could see, and what I saw was a fence. It wasn't just a fence, though. Truthfully speaking, it was the ugliest collection of old rotting wood I had ever seen. It ran about ten feet on either side of the black walnut, and there were pieces sticking up in the air at all kinds of angles.

Sadie let out a whistle and asked exactly what I was thinking, "What in Lord's name is that?"

"It's a spite fence," Pa said as he rubbed his face dry with a cloth.

"A what?"

"A fence folks put up to spite their neighbors. It's on our land, so he can't touch it. Now every time he wants to look at his precious black walnut, he'll see my fence. That will spite him."

"I vow," Sadie said as she pulled me back in the cabin and shut the door, "I don't understand how the Yankees won the war as crazy as they act sometimes. Building a fence just to spite someone."

I agreed with Cousin Sadie about the foolishness of

building an ugly fence. On the other hand, it sure was better than Pa taking the axe to Cutter himself.

———⊷⊶———

After dinner Pa said he didn't feel much like reading the Bible. Sadie said it was just the night the Bible *should* be read in the house, given all the goings-on. I suggested we play dominoes instead, but Sadie said her hands were occupied with her knitting, and we should tell stories.

Pa went first. He told about being a log driver when he was young on the Androscoggin in Maine. He said the fastest way to move logs to the mill was by the river, and every inch of it was covered by hemlock and pine. The driver ran along the shore and loosened any logs that snagged on the bushes. Sometimes the driver rode on the river in a small boat called a bateau and used a long pole to free up logjams. Lose your balance, Pa said, and you could fall out of the bateau, knock your head, and sink under the logs. He saw it happen twice.

Sadie said she didn't have anywheres near as interesting a story to tell as that. But then she remembered how she tamed a rattlesnake once with a bowl of milk, which seemed pretty interesting to me. She told another story about crawling in a cave and getting lost for almost a day in the tunnels. She said the sides of the cave were covered with bats, and the roar of their wings flapping sounded like a waterfall. We have a few bats in our barn, but I couldn't imagine a whole wall of them.

"All right now, your turn," Sadie said to me. "Tell us a story."

I thought back over the last few days, and nothing exciting came to mind except sitting on the hot coals and Licker running over me, which they already knew about. So I thought further back about things I saw on my walks in the woods, and I remembered something so strange that I hadn't told a living soul.

"There were these crows," I said. "I heard them making this terrible noise when I was out in the woods behind Nellie."

"It was a murder of crows," Sadie said.

Pa took the pipe from his mouth. "A murder?"

"That's what they call a group of crows. Like a flock of geese and a herd of cattle. . . ."

". . . and a pack of wolves," Pa said.

Bite raised his head and looked at me, so I tried to think what a group of dogs would be called. All I could come up with was "a bunch of dogs," which didn't sound too good.

"Or a pride of lions," Sadie said.

"And a school of fish," Pa added.

This was getting too much for me. I had to come up with something. "How about a fur full of dogs?"

Sadie looked at me like I'd gone crazy. But then she said, "And a purr full of cats."

That got the two of them laughing so hard that Pa almost choked on his pipe and Sadie just about tipped over her rocker. It didn't seem that funny to me.

"All right," Sadie said after she'd calmed herself, "what about these crows of yours?"

"Well, I was creeping in the woods trying to see what they were yapping about. I figured they were fighting over the carcass of something. I never got close enough to see the whole *murder* of them, but I saw two crows fly to the top of a little hill. Then they rolled over on their backs and slid down on the snow."

Sadie shook her head like I was just fooling with them. Pa kept puffing like he hadn't even heard me.

"It's true," I said. "And when they got to the bottom, they flipped over and flew back up and did it again."

Sadie laughed that big deep ha-ha-ha of hers. "You're pulling my leg, I know it. You think because I'm not from around here I'm not familiar with crows. We have them in North Carolina. They'd eat up a whole pecan orchard if you let them. But they don't do foolish things like sliding down hills."

"I swear I saw it, Sadie."

"Don't you be swearing now," she said.

"I mean I *vow* it's the truth. The crows were having fun, that's what I think."

Pa blew out a big mouthful of smoke. "Birds don't play like that," he said. "It's not the way with wild creatures."

"Bite plays with me. He fetches sticks, doesn't he?"

"That dog ain't wild," Pa said. "Dogs pick things up

from living around us. People are the only ones who play, and mostly young'uns at that."

He put his pipe back in his mouth. I wasn't supposed to say another word. Still, I knew deep inside what I'd seen, and that was two crows playing in the snow.

JUMP

THE SPITE SEEMED to go out of the fence as days passed on and Cutter didn't get riled over it. In fact, Pa was the one who kicked the porch post each time he walked out the front door. I even heard him say a swear, which is something he told me never to do or face a night without supper.

I returned to school, but the truth was I couldn't keep my mind on my workbooks. I got to thinking about how fast things had changed all about me in the last year or so. First Davey went off to The War, then Ma died, and Sadie came to live with us. The house would never be the same without Ma, but I was counting on things getting better when my brother came back. I had lots to show him, like . . .

"Mr. Chance, daydreaming again?"

Miss Whately always called her students Mister and Miss, even the littlest ones in the class, who were only eight years old.

"No, Miss Whately," I said and gathered my books. I knew what was coming.

"You come sit by me," she said, tapping the desk next to hers with her ruler. "Then maybe you'll pay attention to your studies."

"Yes, ma'am," I said as I walked up the aisle. I didn't mind changing desks. I could daydream anywhere about Davey coming home.

⎯⎯⎯⎯•••⎯⎯

On January twelfth, ten days after Spite Fence Day, snow blew down from the north of us and dumped another foot on the ground, which meant I wouldn't be walking to school for a while. The winds sweeping in from Canada froze Pa's fence into one giant icicle. The wood that was meant to look so ugly suddenly appeared kind of strange and beautiful, especially with the sun shining bright.

The day being Sunday, I was free after Bible reading with Sadie and Pa. We only went to proper church in town once a month because it was too cold to ride that far in the wagon in winter. Today the road was blocked altogether. I would get my Sunday lesson at home.

The Bible story that morning was of David slaying Goliath, which was one of my favorites. Sadie read it through and then asked me what the moral of it was. I said, "A body can do anything it sets out to do."

Pa nodded, but Sadie said that David had the Lord behind him, that's why he was powerful. A body could try as hard as he pleased and still fail, she said, if the Lord wasn't with him.

I wished to have the Lord behind me that very morning, because I had something frightening I was going to do: jump!

Every boy in these parts jumps from their second floor when they reach twelve years old. Pa said boys have been doing it since he was little. After he said this he waved his big hand in the air saying that didn't mean me because I'd probably break a leg and be useless for chores around the house and have to face his belt in the bargain. I didn't fancy the strap on my backside. But still, I couldn't think of anything Pa could threaten me with that would keep me from jumping. It was just something a boy had to do.

I'd been waiting all winter for the perfect snow. Davey said you wanted a foot of fresh snow overtop a couple of feet of packed snow. That way you were sure to land soft. When I looked outside from the front window, that's what I saw: new snow rising right up to the sill.

So after we finished with David and Goliath I pulled on three pairs of socks and Davey's knee-high boots and two pairs of Pa's old mittens and my red cap with the drop ears and Davey's jacket and Ma's long scarf. Pa passed me in the kitchen and said it was right democratic the way I borrowed something from everybody rather than all from one. He asked me where I was off to and I just said "outside," which was true. Then Sadie came downstairs looking at me like she knew I was up to no good but she couldn't tell exactly what kind of no good it was.

I went up to my room and closed the door behind me. Then I pushed up the window, which was awful hard to do being just about frozen. I got it open wide enough to stick my head out, and the air felt cold as ice on my face. Down below me was nothing but white. It looked like clouds, but I knew it was harder than it seemed.

I pulled my head back in and pushed the window up higher and I stuck one leg out. Then I swung the other over the ledge, and there I was sitting in my window, holding on to the inside. Suddenly I thought maybe this wasn't the best day to be jumping. What if I did fall wrong and broke my leg or knocked my head? Pa or Sadie wouldn't even know I was out there. I could freeze myself into an icicle before they found me. It made more sense to jump when someone else was there, like Davey. It would be more fun, too, being watched.

I started to pull myself back inside when I said to myself, "Jeremy Chance, if you're too scared to jump, just say you're too scared and go on about your day. But don't go pretending you want to wait just to show off to Davey."

I sat there for a few seconds, half in and half out, not feeling inclined altogether one way or the other. It seemed to me that I was thinking too much about this. I remembered Davey saying that sometimes you had to just stop thinking and throw yourself into a situation no matter the consequences. He said there was *good scared* that kept you from doing stuff that could get yourself killed and *bad scared* that kept you from trying new things. I figured that right then I was in the grip of bad scared and the only thing to do about it was yell "Bombs Away!" and push myself off.

Suddenly I was in the air, like someone had pulled the world out from under my feet. I felt like a bird—but not a bird soaring over the land. I felt like a bird shot out of the sky and falling fast. I crashed into the ground feet first and tried to roll, like Davey told me. But my legs sank so far into the snow that I was standing straight, buried up to my chest. I'd lost my cap in the air and my ears were stinging from the cold, but otherwise I was fine. I'd done it, jumped from the second floor like Davey did, and three months younger, too!

"What in Lord's name?" Sadie burst out the front door looking at me with such a confusion on her face as I'd ever seen. Pa was right behind her. "I was looking out the window," she said, "and all of a sudden a body comes dropping past. My heart stopped, I swear it did," she said, clutching her chest.

Pa laughed at her fright, and that made Sadie mad.

"You laughing at that boy of yours falling out a window? Could have killed himself and scared a woman to her death. That would have been two bodies to deal with in one morning."

Pa wiped his face of his grin. "Guess we should have warned you, Sadie, but I didn't know the boy had it in him already. Jeremy didn't fall. It's a tradition in these parts to jump into the snow about his age. Davey jumped some years back. I jumped myself from that same window when I was a boy. My pa did the same. The snow gets so deep up here year after year, you just can't keep looking out at it without jumping once in your life."

Sadie shook her head. "I don't know if it's the cold up north or what that makes people crazy. But I'll tell you, I ain't tending that boy if he's hurt. He can crawl to do his chores if he has to." With that Sadie turned back and hurried in the house.

"You break anything, Jeremy?" Pa asked me.

"Don't think so."

He stepped into the snow a little ways and reached out his hand. I took it and he yanked me free. As we went inside, he patted me on the back a few times like knocking off the snow or congratulating me, I couldn't tell which.

I kept out of Sadie's way the rest of the morning. The sun warmed the day to near thawing temperature, and that's when I headed back outside to make some snow figures. This time I left by the front door.

I was pretty fair at making figures. I won a blue ribbon at the Derry festival two winters ago with Davey. We shaped a big humpback whale eating a man. Neither of us had ever seen a whale, but we had a picture that Miss Whately from school gave us from the *National Geographic*. We had to imagine the eating-a-man part, which was easy because we just thought of Jonah in the Bible.

The trick to making things out of snow is to catch it on the melting side of noon when it's soft enough to mold. Bite came out to join me, so of course the first figure I had to make was of the finest looking collie ever born. He expected me to play with him the whole time, too, so I had to keep throwing snowballs in the air to busy him. He'd leap up to catch the snowball between his teeth, and each time it broke in his mouth he got this crazy look of surprise on his face, like maybe he was expecting something white and soft, such as marshmallow. He kept barking for more though.

After I finished shaping the dog, I called Bite over to see it, and he sniffed all around and started barking like it was a wolf come around the house. I grabbed him and we wrestled around for a while, knocking over my snow dog. I lay there for a minute as if I was hurt, and he barked even louder, calling for help like I taught him. Then he settled next to me, keeping me warm, and I could feel his heart pounding loud as iron to an anvil. I opened one eye to sneak a look, and Bite saw me and started grinning. I swear he did.

Then I jumped up and raced him to the back door. He beat me as always and sat there on the step wagging his tail waiting for me. Before we went in I made him sit while I dug ice from between his paws. That way Sadie wouldn't sweep the broom at him for dripping across the floor. Besides, Bite didn't like ice in his paws.

Inside, the chills hit me all of a sudden, and there was only one thing to stoke up my insides: hot apple cider, vinegar, and honey. We rarely had cider or honey, but I knew who did: Cutter.

So I left Bite to lie in front of the fire and headed out the front door again to go next door. I had to stomp out a new path in the fresh snow. When I got to Pa's fence I slipped through an open space like I was a spy sneaking through German territory. I crawled on my belly the rest of the way, with bullets whizzing over my head.

The door opened before I even knocked, and there was old man Cutter leaning on his cane, with a blanket around his shoulders. "I saw you coming from my window," he said. "You figuring on attacking this place?"

"Yes sir," I said and aimed my arms at him like a rifle. "Your life or your apple cider."

"Cider's probably worth more," he said. I moved inside and shut the door behind me. "I was wondering if you'd be coming over here again," he said.

"Why wouldn't I be coming over, Mr. Cutter?"

He nodded out the window where the spite fence ran smack up to his black walnut. "Your pa's powerful angered at me. He still let you come over?"

"He didn't say I couldn't. I've just been busy the last few days."

"Then help these old bones to the fire."

I hurried to lend him a hand. My arm just about circled his shoulders and touched myself again. Cutter was always "old man Cutter" to Davey and me, but now he was really looking old, like a deer skin that's been hung out and dried too long. His face was sunk in, and the veins in his ears stood out clear and purple.

"I suppose you think me contrary, like your pa does?" he said as he mixed up the cider and vinegar, two parts to one. He set the pan of it on his stove.

"You ain't never been contrary to me, Mr. Cutter."

"You don't hold with all your pa's opinions?"

That sounded like a question I couldn't get right answering either way. "Mostly I do," I said, finding some middle ground, "at least the ones where he seems right."

Cutter stuck his hands over the pan to warm them up. "When I was your age my papa was always right no matter if he was wrong, if you see my meaning. It's a pleasure knowing a young'un who learns to see right from wrong through his own eyes." Cutter took down his huge jar of honey from the shelf and poured some into the pan. "Your pa is as stubborn as a hen turkey who won't come out of a storm. But down under I think he ain't so ornery as he makes out sometimes. You respect him."

"Yes sir, I do that."

"But you respect yourself at the same time. That's the trick."

The apple cider, vinegar, and honey was boiling up now, steaming the room in a sweet smell. Cutter took a mug off the hook on the wall and poured for me.

"You aren't taking any?" I asked as I stirred up the hot drink.

He shook his head and made his way back toward his chair by the window. "Can't say I've felt much like treating myself the last week or so. When you're nearing four score years like me, things don't roll off you so easy. I never had bad blood with no man before this with your pa. It runs against my grain."

I gulped down the cider and poured myself another

mug. Cutter always said I needn't ask. Standing there drinking like that, my eyes started wandering around the cabin. There were empty bean cans and cracker tins on his table. There was an empty cornmeal bag and a box of salt codfish on the floor. There were hammers and nails, a canvas sheet, pages from a book, and a shining silver girding chain for measuring oxen, a creature Cutter hadn't kept for years. It seemed like all of his life was tossed about for anyone to walk on. He never lived like this when Mrs. Cutter was alive. What I wondered was, had he always wanted to live like this or not?

"If you don't mind my saying so, Mr. Cutter, you could use some help cleaning up your place. I'm offering myself."

He stared at me like he heard but didn't exactly understand.

"I don't mean for money," I said.

"You see, boy," Cutter started up again, "if your pa had just asked why I wouldn't sell the tree, if he had just listened to reason. Folks don't care for sentiment anymore. You remember that word, sentiment."

"What's it mean?"

"It means feeling strong about something that's close to you. That's what me and Heddie had between us. I courted her under that walnut out there, got my first kiss from her. We shaded under it in the summer. There isn't a cooler spot in miles." Cutter wiped his eyes with the back of his hand. "And I buried her there," he said, as if whispering me a secret. I guess he forgot that we were standing over the grave next to him when they put the box in.

"I cut the weeds around her all summer," he said. "Come fall I spread the leaves over her like a quilt. Each spring that walnut comes to life again, and it's like seeing her come alive." Cutter looked over at me, but his eyes were cloudy, like he couldn't see through them. "Boy, The War just finished in Europe, but there's war still going on here."

"There's war around here, Mr. Cutter?"

He nodded. "Wars aren't just between countries. They can be between two people, too."

"You mean Pa's warring with you?" It sure seemed a strange way to think of things.

"That he is. War ain't uniforms or cannon or armies. War is one man hating another enough to take up against him. Your pa wouldn't take his rifle and shoot me cold, but I think right today he hates me so much he wishes me dead. War ain't nothing more than hate with a rifle in its hand."

I wanted to tell Cutter that Pa didn't have any such thing on his mind, but I didn't know that for sure. I finished my hot cider and set the mug on the table. "I guess I better go, Mr. Cutter. Pa will be wondering where I got to."

"You're a good listener, boy," he said, "not jumpy like most young'uns. I'm pleased to have you visit any time."

"I'll come again soon," I said and opened the door. Then I remembered my big news. "I jumped today, Mr. Cutter, from my window." I spread my arms like wings and flapped them so he'd get the picture.

"Did you now?" he said.

"I did . . . three months younger than Davey. Wait till I tell him."

"He'll be proud of you," Cutter said. "I'm sure of it."

I had never thought about that before—Davey proud of me! That would be something.

I left Cutter's cabin and looked toward home. All I could see ahead of me was Pa's spite fence.

WHIPPING

WHEN I GOT HOME from Cutter's, Pa was gone and Sadie was gone and Bite, too. The place felt empty.

I was trying to think of something interesting to do when I saw a letter on the table. I could tell right off it was from Davey because of the strange stamps on the envelope. I held it up to the light, but I couldn't read anything inside.

This was an awful maddening situation: a letter from Davey, and Pa not there to open it. I looked at the front again: "To Jack Chance (and Jeremy)." My name was on the same line as Pa's. That meant I had just as much right to open it as he did, right?

I sat down in Ma's rocker and slipped my finger under the flap. It took some coaxing, but finally the envelope popped open without ripping. I took out the letter and read:

Dear Pa and Jeremy and Ma in Heaven,

Your letter caught up with me a day ago, and I wish I could have forever stayed a step ahead of

*such mournful news. Our captain always said
to think of home and your mother every day. I
did that, but I didn't know to fear for her dying,
and now she's gone.*

*I got my orders to head home. The ship with
the wounded from the Yankee 26th should be
pulling in to Boston about the 15th of January,
and I'll take the train up to Derry. They're giving each soldier a coat, shoes, and a sixty-dollar
bonus. Imagine, Pa, sixty dollars! I suppose you
got some ideas what to do with that.*

*It will be a strange and wonderful thing re-
turning to a peaceful place. I've seen so much of
France dug up by bombs that it makes me sick
thinking that people are doing this.*

*I've made some fast friends in the 26th, good
boys from Downeast and the Green Mountains.
During fighting you understand that any second they might take a bullet and be gone, so you
try not to know anybody too close. But you can't
sleep under the same blankets and drink from
the same jug without making friends. You pray
for yourself and you pray for them to make it
through each day. The only one I didn't know I
needed to pray for was Ma, and now you tell me
The Influenza took her. I remember she said she'd
give her right arm to bring me home safe from
The War. Now I'm coming home and I'd give my
one good arm to have her there meeting me.*

With luck and a good trip across the ocean,
I'll be returned well in time for the first sugar-
off. Some nights I get to dreaming about lying
back in the snow under Grandpa's maple. I
dream of tapping that tree and letting the sap
drip down into my mouth. You and me, Jeremy,
will do it all morning—at least until Pa calls us
to chores.

Keep me in your dreams a little while longer
and I'll be home to you.

Your Son and Brother,
Davey Chance

P.S. Can't wait to meet Pa's cousin Sadie, hol-
lerin' and all.

That letter was just like Davey. It made me wet in the eyes missing him bad. Pa said no one likes seeing a man crying in the open, so I kept it inside most of the time. But thinking how Davey could have died from a bullet scared me something awful. It didn't always seem so at the time, but an older brother was a handy thing to have. He made growing up a whole lot easier for me, since he'd gone through it already himself.

A noise upstairs made me jump, and I tried to slide the letter back into the envelope just as Sadie started down the steps.

"Thought I heard someone down here, unless the mice have taken to wearing boots." She laughed when she said this and held her stomach, like it might fall out of her.

I knew it was a little joke, and people meant you to laugh along with them. But I wasn't much for doing that unless it was a real knee-slapper. So I faked a little laugh and said, "No ma'am, I ain't seen no critters in boots 'round here."

"Except a little critter named Jeremy. Now where did you get to this morning?"

I didn't want to tell her 'cause she might tell Pa. But I couldn't lie, either. "Nowhere special," I said.

She leaned over a little to look at me closer, and I moved my arms to cover the letter. "Where's nowhere special?"

"Not far," I said. "Kind of near nowhere at all."

"I can see I'm not going to get a straight answer from you," she said and straightened up again. Then she reached down and picked up my arm. There was the letter, sticking half out of the envelope. "So that's what you've been up to—reading other people's mail."

"It's to me, too, Cousin Sadie, take a look." I held up the envelope and pointed at my name.

"It's to your pa first," she said. "You know he's supposed to be the first one to read a letter. That's why I set it out for him. You can never tell what kind of news might be coming in it."

"How come we got a letter on Sunday?"

"Because Mr. Harley from the post office brought it out himself. He thought it might be important." Sadie stared at the envelope for a moment. "Well, it looks like the damage is already done," she said and pulled up a chair next to mine. "I might as well take a peek myself."

I handed over the letter and she read it to herself. "Why, the fifteenth," she said, "that's just three days from now. This house will be bursting with life again."

When she finished she folded the paper neatly back into its envelope, then took it to the kitchen. She ran a little water in a cup and stirred in a tablespoon of baking soda. Then she scooped out a bit of the paste on her finger and wiped it onto the envelope. She pressed the flap down for a few seconds with the palms of her hands, and when she let go it stayed shut.

"There," she said, "no use giving your pa something else to be upset about. Now run this over to him. He got called to Lucy Thompson's on an emergency of some sort. Just follow Possum Road north toward . . ."

"Sadie," I said, "I've only been living in Derry for about twelve years longer than you. I know the Thompson place."

"Then what are you waiting for?" she said and swatted at my backside.

I grabbed Davey's jacket from the door hook and was outside in a second. I dashed up Possum Road as if German Fokkers were dive-bombing low overhead and buzzing the snow with bullets. I turned up my collar and zigzagged down the road till I reached Colson's farm. There I leaped a snow bunker and weaved a trail through the evergreens that nobody knew but me and the deer.

I came out of the woods at the rear of Thompson's and

ran around to the front—there was Pa! The hammer
slipped in his hand, and he jumped about as high as the
hayloft, holding his finger.

"What in tarnation?" he yelled and stuck his hand in
the snow to freeze out the pain. "Why don't you give a
body some notice when you're coming, boy?"

"Sorry, Pa," I said, "I didn't see you."

He picked up the nail from the snow and commenced
to hammering again. I pulled the letter from my pocket
and waved it in the air. "It's Davey, Pa, he's . . . he's written
another letter."

"Why didn't you say so?" Pa took the letter from me
and read it lickety-split. That's where I get my fast reading
from. I watched his face as he read, and I could tell by
how he lighted up that he couldn't wait for Davey to come
home, just like me.

That letter put Pa in a good mood. He finished up at
Thompson's and we walked home together. Sadie greeted
us with the smell of applesauce cake, and she cut us each
a slice as a celebration of the good news. Everything was
perfect at that moment.

I'm not exactly sure how things went from perfect to
terrible so fast, but they did. All I remember is that we
were eating the cake, and I told Pa he was wrong.

I can't believe I said it. I know I shouldn't have. What
happened is that on the way in the house Pa noticed my

footprints in the snow heading from our door to Cutter's. When we sat down to the applesauce cake, he asked if I'd been over there. I said yes. He asked if Cutter had come to his senses, and I said that the spite fence was making him feel real bad. Then I said, "When are you going to take it down, Pa?"

He said, "Why would I take it down?"

"Well," I said, "because it's . . . wrong." That was the only word I could think of.

He scraped the last crumbs of his cake off his plate and said, "I'm the one who put it up, you remember that?"

"Sure, Pa."

"So you're saying I was wrong for doing it?"

At the time it seemed like a simple question, and I nodded like I would to a hundred other things he asked me.

Pa looked at me like I was some strange creature that had crawled out of the woods, and he didn't recognize what it was. He repeated his question, "You're saying I'm wrong for putting up the spite fence?" He rubbed his hands together when he said this, which made the muscles in his arms look even bigger than they were.

"No, Pa, I didn't say that exactly."

"What did you say, *exactly?*"

I tried to find some way to say that the fence was wrong without actually saying he was wrong for putting it up. I sure wished I were better with words so that I could say one thing and mean another. I ended up not saying anything.

"Well," Pa said, "are you man enough to stand by your words?"

When he put it that way, there was only one thing I could answer. "Yes sir."

"Yes sir what?"

"Yes sir, I'm man enough to stand by my words."

"Which words?"

"I guess the ones that said you were wrong about the fence."

"You guess?"

"No, I don't guess. I said it."

Pa nodded that he understood me perfectly now. I thought maybe he'd be proud that I was standing my ground for what I believed. But he said, "Now that we both know what you said and what you meant, I'm giving you the chance to take back your words." His voice wasn't loud or angry, and that scared me, because he sounded like some other man, not Pa at all. "Are you taking back your words?"

I couldn't figure out what to do. If I took back my words, he'd think I was just a little one who couldn't stand up for what he believed. But if I kept on saying he was wrong, who knew what he'd do to me? It wasn't a circumstance that had ever happened before.

Pa pushed his chair away from the table.

"Ah, Pa?" I said backing away.

"Yes?"

"I'm not meaning to cross you. It's just I heard Cutter's

side today, and maybe if you did, too, you'd feel the same way as me."

"You remember me walking over to his place to talk about the tree?"

"Yes, Pa."

"You think I didn't listen to him?"

"I'm sure you listened, Pa."

"I listened, and I didn't like what I heard. You like everything you hear, boy?"

"No, Pa."

"Now, I'm asking you again, you still say I'm wrong?"

My mouth felt like it was stuffed with cotton. I couldn't say a word. I closed my eyes and called up all the nerve I had in me. I nodded.

A loud thump jolted my eyes open. Pa's fist had slammed down on the table. Then his hands were on me, jerking me into the air as if I had no more weight to me than a Teddy bear. He slipped me over his hip like a sack of flour and carried me out the front door toward the barn. As he went his free hand loosened the strap of his belt.

I knew for sure my time had come. Not to die, mind you. Pa's strap on your backside didn't kill you. It just made you wish to die. I hadn't had the displeasure of it myself, but I sure heard Davey getting it the night he rode Licker against Pa's wishes.

Pa had to drop me to the ground at the barn so he could use his two hands to pull open the door that always stuck in winter. I could have run from him then, but where would I go in the cold of January? Who would take me in knowing I was Pa's boy? And once he caught up with me, the punishment would be worse than I was in for already.

Pa swung the old door wide open and tapped my shoulder to go in. He lit the lantern on the hook, and the shed lit up like so many other times when we came in here together. I'd sweep out the stalls or groom Licker while he sharpened his tools and laid them out for his next day's work. Sometimes he sanded down a piece of wood. Pa wasn't a man who talked much normally. But working in the barn after dinner, I'd ask him about the old days, and he could talk for hours, which made my chores go fast. He told me about how he ran off with the Four Paw Circus when it cleared out of Derry one night. He was just sixteen. He spent three months cleaning the animal cages and watering the elephants. One time Buffalo Bill appeared at the circus and shot a hole through a silver dollar he tossed in the air. Pa made running away sound awfully exciting.

But my favorite story he told was about joining Teddy Roosevelt's Rough Riders and charging up San Juan Hill in Puerto Rico. He said no man lived more straight and brave than Teddy.

Those were wonderful times when we came to the barn and talked, and I thought I'd try asking Pa a question about Teddy to get his mind off the whipping. But just as I opened my mouth, he said, "Take off your jacket, Jeremy. And mind you fold it nice." When I did that he said, "Now lower your britches. No use messing a good pair."

I took my time, hoping that maybe something would

61

happen outside, like Sadie calling or lightning striking or an earthquake—I'd learned about them in school. I wished for anything that would take Pa's attention away. I closed my eyes and promised the Lord an extra hour's Bible reading every night before bed if he'd just make something happen.

Nothing did. I guess it's like Sadie says, the Lord has more important things to do than answer every little request by every boy in the world.

Pa pointed to his work table, and I hobbled over there with my britches around my ankles. "Lean over it," he said, and I did. I closed my eyes and heard his belt whip through the air. But I didn't feel anything. I thought maybe he had taken me out here just to scare me, which he sure had. I wouldn't be telling Pa he was wrong again anytime soon. I started to raise up, and then I heard another whip of the leather. A second later it stung my backside like a pack of yellow jackets. I felt like screaming. I felt like falling into the dirt on the floor and rubbing out the pain. I felt like cussing, and not just the worm-eating Huns, either. I felt like cussing Pa. But I remembered Davey's words after he took his first licking: "You can't let on that it hurts," he said. "Pa goes harder on you if you whine about it."

So I stuffed the sleeve of my jacket in my mouth to make sure no sound could come from it. And I stiffened my legs so they wouldn't buckle under me. Pa whipped me three more times. With each stroke I told myself that I'd never let him do this to me again.

WRONG

I DIDN'T SIT MUCH the next day. Sadie found all kinds of standing-up chores for me to do, like sweeping out the house and dusting the jars sitting on the kitchen shelves. It seemed to me I was being punished twice: first the whipping and now the extra chores. But I didn't complain for fear Pa would hear and find a third way of punishing me.

I tried to stay out of his way. Still, he snapped at me a few times for doing something he didn't like or not doing something he wanted done. You could get in trouble with him both ways on days that he was already angry at you.

It seemed to me that I should be steaming angry at him for whipping me when I didn't do any more than speak my mind. Wasn't that one thing we fought the Germans for, to live free? What good was living free if you couldn't say what you thought?

Pa walked over to the Johnson place late afternoon to collect some money he was owed, and Sadie said I could go outside for a while. But by then the sun was already going down and it was colder than Bite's nose, which I know because he kept sticking it in my face. I went outside anyway and threw snowballs at the side of the barn. I made a perfect circle of snow marks around the window. That wasn't easy to do because one missed throw and my snowball would have sailed right through the glass. I knew I was tempting another whipping, and it was kind of exciting, especially with Bite jumping and barking at every throw.

When my arm got tired I decided I'd head over to Cutter's. Pa was in town, so it seemed like the perfect time.

I knocked on the old man's door, and after a little shuffling I heard him say, "Come in."

"Hello, Mr. Cutter," I said, and he nodded to me from the shadows of his room.

"Have a seat, boy, take the load off."

"I don't feel the inclination to sit, if you don't mind." I rubbed the backside of my trousers and figured he'd get my point.

"Crossed your pa, huh? That happens from time to time. You'll get over the ache. It goes pretty fast."

"It isn't the ache, Mr. Cutter. I don't mind that so much."

"What is it then?"

"A pa shouldn't be whipping his boy just for speaking his mind. That don't seem right."

The old man nodded. "I agree with you there. What exactly did you say to him?"

"Well, I guess I told him he was wrong."

"Wrong?"

I nodded.

"That's a strong thing to say to your father."

"I know."

"I don't suppose he took it well."

"He took his belt to me, that's what he took. First time he ever did that."

"Your pa doesn't punish you or your brother over every little thing, as far as I can tell. He must have been sore upset at hearing his youngest say he was wrong."

"He was upset all right."

"How many times he swing the belt at you?"

"Four times, and not *that* hard, really. I mean, I didn't bleed or anything."

"He didn't want to hurt you bad, just teach you a lesson that it isn't right for a boy to tell a father he's wrong."

"Even if he *is* wrong?"

Cutter shrugged and stirred the cup of tea sitting on the table in front of him. It smelled like cinnamon. "That isn't an easy question to answer," he said. "A boy should say what's right as he sees it, but he shouldn't be disrespectful to his pa."

I nodded at his description of the problem and waited for him to tell me what the answer was. But he just sipped his tea, not saying anything. I figured that if as old as he was, Cutter hadn't figured out the answer, there mustn't be one. I'd either have to speak my mind and take the whipping, or keep my mouth shut, which I wasn't very good at doing.

"You ever have trouble with your own pa, Mr. Cutter?"

The old man started laughing so hard that he had to

grab hold of his chair to keep himself from falling over. "Why, boy, my father and me had run-ins every other day from the time I started in long pants till I turned sixteen."

"What happened then? You get so big he wouldn't touch you?"

Cutter shook his head. "I knew I'd never grow that big. So I just up and left the house."

"You ran away?"

"That I did. A few years later the war started, and I signed myself into the Union Army and headed off to fight the Rebs."

I couldn't believe it, old man Cutter a Yankee soldier fighting hand to hand against the rebels. Why hadn't he told me this before? I would have asked him all about Gettysburg and Bull Run and whether he served under Grant or heard Abe Lincoln speak. The Civil War was my favorite subject in school. There was a war a boy could do something in. You didn't have to worry about planes dropping bombs on you or tanks rolling over you.

"Worst fool thing I ever did," Cutter said. "It was a miserable war. I'd rather have taken ten whippings a day than fight an hour at Gettysburg."

I couldn't imagine anything worse than ten whippings a day. "What do you mean, Mr. Cutter?"

"I mean it was slaughter. I saw bodies falling on top of bodies. Men were stealing boots and jackets off the dead. There weren't enough doctors or medicine, so the wounded tried to walk home on their own. I saw one soldier carrying his arm wrapped up like a loaf of bread."

That didn't sound like the Civil War that I'd read about in school. I was going to ask Cutter more about it when the door flew open, and there was Pa.

"Come out here, Jeremy," he said.

I jumped up and ran over to him. Pa nabbed me by my jacket collar. "This boy won't be bothering you no more."

"He ain't no bother," Cutter said.

"Just the same, he won't be coming over no more." With that Pa shoved the door shut and hauled me over the snow back home.

When we got inside our cabin and hung up our coats, I tried explaining how Cutter was just telling me about the Civil War. Pa said, "You're learning stuff there you shouldn't be learning."

"I was just learning about how bad the fighting was. Mr. Cutter says . . ."

Pa shook me by the arm. "I don't care what he says. What I say is that you stay away from his place."

"You mean the rest of the day?"

"Stay away until I tell you."

I could have understood if he'd said one day or two days or even three. But "until I tell you" could be weeks or months. "Pa?" I said, but he turned on me quickly and waved his big finger in the air. That meant don't say another word.

Well, maybe he could stop me talking, but he couldn't stop me from thinking, and what I thought was that Pa was being wrong again. First he was wrong for putting up the spite fence, then he was wrong for whipping me, and now he was wrong for keeping me from seeing Cutter. A couple weeks before it had been fine for me to visit him, so I didn't see why I shouldn't now. It was neighborly to visit, especially someone shut in by the snow. He needed me to pump water for him sometimes and fetch him food from his cellar. An old man could die if he couldn't get food and water.

Then it struck me—maybe Pa wanted Cutter to die. I didn't like thinking that. A tree couldn't be worth the life of a person. But that's the way Pa seemed to be thinking of this black walnut.

———

I headed up to bed early. Sadie said I must be sick wanting to go to sleep so soon. She put her hand on my forehead and declared it hot. Of course, I'd just been leaning toward the fire, so naturally my face was flush.

I started for the steps, and she said, "Aren't you forgetting something?"

I wasn't forgetting. I was going upstairs without giving Pa his kiss. I didn't even feel like saying good night to him. I figured that would show him how mad I was. But now that Sadie had made a point of it, I couldn't rightly go through with my plan. It was one thing to disrespect somebody when you could pretend later that you forgot. It was another thing to disrespect him when he was looking at you straightaway from his rocker, as Pa was now. So I walked back to him and put my arms around his shoulders and touched my face next to his rough skin. I didn't squeeze him like usual, and I didn't say "I love you, Pa," in his ear like usual. I didn't say anything.

He said, "Night, boy," like I was some young'un who just happened to be staying over, not his special youngest son.

I couldn't sleep. The wind started howling up outside, and it sounded like some hungry creature trying to get in. I pulled my blanket tight about my neck and thought over the last two weeks. It seemed to me that something had happened to change Pa, and that thing was his want of the black walnut on Cutter's land. He had always taught me that wanting something so bad could twist you up inside, and here it was happening to him.

I knew about wanting. I'd been looking at the Spring Steel Coaster in our new Sears Roebuck and Co. catalog for months. But I didn't want it so much that I'd ruin a neighbor over it. It seemed to me that Pa was acting worse than a little one who gets angry when he doesn't get his way. Then something Cutter said came to me, how he'd had run-ins with his own pa and finally took off to get away from him. If Cutter could do it, why couldn't I? I sure had reason enough. It wasn't bearable living with a pa who could drag you off to the shed for a whipping any time he didn't like your opinion.

The problem was, where would I run to? It didn't take

me long to figure out there was only one place to go: to Boston to meet Davey. He said in his letter his ship was due in January fifteenth, and that was Wednesday. Davey would know how to fix things between me and Pa, I was sure of it.

After I solved the first problem, a second problem occurred to me. How would I pay to get to Boston? There were twenty-five cents sitting in my top drawer under my wool socks. I'd been saving that toward buying the coaster. I also had the 1906 silver half-dollar Pa gave me to honor the year I was born. But I'd vowed to him that I'd never spend such a wonderful present. No matter how mad I was at Pa, I couldn't go back on a vow.

Twenty-five cents seemed like a lot of money to me. But would it take me all the way to Boston? I had no idea, and Davey wasn't there to ask.

RUNNING

I DECIDED TO SEE just how far my two bits would take me. The next day I jumped out of bed and was dressed before Pa even turned into my room. He said, "Good boy," which he never said to me in the morning before. I thought, if I was so good, why did he whip me?

We ate bread and jam together at the table. Pa sat across from me and didn't say anything. I didn't say anything. As usual, Sadie did enough talking for all three of us. She said how she was going to be making pies all morning and then take them to the shut-ins. Pa grunted at that. I would have bet he was thinking the same as me— don't forget to leave one of those pies home. She went on about how the stove wasn't heating right and the roof was leaking again so Pa had better climb up and knock the snow off before it all came dripping inside the house. Pa grunted to everything, then wiped his chin and said he'd get to it when the time came. Sadie said we could be in knee-deep water before Time came. She made it sound like "Time" was a person. Sadie was the only one I ever saw who could get away speaking to him like that. Even my ma held her tongue around him.

"The road's just about clear all the way to Derry," he said. "You can make it to school tomorrow, Jeremy."

I nodded, but he must not have seen me.

"You hear?"

"Yes, Pa, the road will be clear enough for me to go to school tomorrow."

"By rights you could walk it today."

I nodded again. I was going to walk that road today, but not to the schoolhouse.

After Pa left I did my morning chores and then sat next to the stove whittling a fine piece of ash I found in the wood-pile. It was about as long as my hand and as wide as my wrist. As soon as I saw this wood I thought "sparrow." I don't mean the piece looked like the bird on the outside. But inside the wood I saw a sparrow waiting to come out. Sometimes I could look at a piece of wood all day and see nothing but wood. This time I saw a bird.

So I started whittling. Sadie was baking her pies, and the whole house smelled wonderful. She let me eat some of the filling, which I licked off her big wooden spoon. It was so good I said, "Why do you bother making the pie, Sadie? The filling is perfect."

"Any woman can stir up filling," she said. "Only a few know how to make the whole pie."

Sitting there whittling and smelling pies, I almost forgot what I'd decided: I was going to run away. It was almost as if Sadie knew what I was thinking and was tempting me. . . . *Why do you want to leave your nice warm home, Jeremy, where there's blueberry pie—your favorite—baking in the oven?*

The preacher at church said one time that Temptation took many forms, and I figured it was taking the form of blueberry pie today. But I was watching out for Temptation, just like he said to do. So when Sadie offered to let me swipe my hand around the blueberry bowl again, I said, "No thanks." She was sure surprised.

After Sadie left with her basketful of pies to deliver to the shut-ins, I put on two pairs of socks and two sweaters and two pairs of gloves and two scarves and two of my thickest winter pants. I figured if I fell over in the snow like that I wouldn't freeze for days.

I kissed Bite good-bye and told him not to let on which direction I was heading. I knew he'd be watching me from the window. I said good-bye to Licker, too, and true to her name she gave me a big lick on the side of my face. I thought about saying good-bye to Cutter, but I figured that was the first place Pa would go looking for me. I couldn't ask Cutter to lie for me. It was better he didn't know anything.

It was four miles and thirty-two feet to town. Davey

figured the distance. One day he counted his steps from our front door to the railroad station and multiplied that number by the length of each step. Then he divided by the number of feet in a mile. He could do stuff like that. He was careful to make each step the same length and walk in a straight line. Me? I was weaving all over the road as usual. Sometimes I ran a little. Sometimes I walked backward because I always thought where you've been could be just as interesting as where you were going. Sometimes I skipped a few steps or walked sideways. You could never measure a mile by me.

About halfway to town I passed the Curley house. It was hard to sneak past there without being seen because one of the eleven Curley kids was always outside. I knew the names of every one of them, but sometimes I couldn't remember which name went with which face. This day two of the younger ones were outside throwing snowballs at each other. I think it was Charlie and Jack, but it could have been Jack and Samuel or even Samuel and Charlotte because she was ten and looked like a boy when she had on winter clothes.

I tried bending low behind the snowbank, but still one of them saw me and called out, "Hey, Chance, come on over. We're playing war."

I waved and shook my head. "Going some place," I called back.

"Where you going?" he said.

"*Some* place," I yelled again, and by then I was past their house.

You would have thought that all of Derry was on the road that day. Mr. Junkett "the Younger" pulled up to me in his carriage and asked if I wanted a ride. I did, but if I sat next to him he'd be asking all sorts of questions that I didn't feel like answering. So I said no thanks, that walking suited me fine.

Two women I had never seen before passed me and nodded.

"Fine day," I said, which is what my pa always said to strangers.

Mr. Crockett, the rag man, stopped his wagon to talk to me. Ma used to give him the rags she didn't need any more, and a couple of times I saw her slip in one that had barely been used. He'd tip his hat to her when she did that.

"Forget which way your house is, Jeremy?"

"No, sir," I said, "I'm just out stretching my legs." That's something else Pa used to say when he was tired of sitting and got up to go outside for a walk.

"Your legs don't look like they need any stretching to me," Mr. Crockett said. "They already reach the ground."

He laughed so hard that he pulled on the reins to Max, and the old horse reared up his head and opened his mouth like he was laughing, too.

"That's a good one," I said and kept on toward town.

I never saw any man like him. He was tall and skinny with bushy hair, kind of like the scarecrow Mr. Shaw puts out in his cornfield each spring. He was dressed in black trousers and a light black jacket and a black top hat, a real proper man. But his hands were wrapped in rags, and newspaper was sticking out of his shoes. He was standing about ten feet off to the side of the railroad tracks, and I figured he was waiting for the next train of coal to round the bend out of Derry. A few pieces always fell off, enough sometimes for a fire.

As I got closer I saw that his head was tilted back. He was staring up into the sky. I walked up next to him and looked up, too, but it was almost dark now and I couldn't see anything. Finally I couldn't help but ask, "What are you looking at, mister?"

He didn't move his head. "I believe I heard one of those airplanes."

"So? You can see airplanes almost any day over Derry."

"Ah, my boy," he said looking down at me now, "you were born after the invention of the flying machine, so to you it's nothing special. To me, flying is magical."

"Well, I don't hear anything."

"I suppose you're right," he said and commenced to walking down the tracks, away from the station.

Then I did hear something, a strange rustling sound coming from the man. "What's that?"

He turned around. "What's what?"

"When you walk, the rustling."

He opened his jacket, and inside were wads of newspaper stuffed in his trousers and sticking out of his shirt. "Newspaper," he said, "it makes a wonderful insulator."

I had never seen newspaper used for anything but reading or starting a fire. This man was wearing it like clothes. "What's an insulator?"

"An insulator keeps the heat of your body in and the cold out."

A large headline caught my eye, the biggest I'd ever seen: "Roosevelt Dead!" I pointed at the man's chest. "Teddy's dead?"

He nodded at me. "Didn't you hear? He died about a week ago."

Teddy Roosevelt dead! Pa must not have known either or he would have told us. "My pa says Teddy was the best president we ever had, even better than Lincoln because Teddy was a Rough Rider and fought in the Spanish-American War. My pa did, too. He even grew his mustache like Teddy's."

"Teddy was a good one, that's for sure," the man said. Suddenly he squatted down in the snow and patted the spot next to him on the bank. "Sit a spell, if you have a mind to," he said.

I sat next to him and smelled something rotten. "Did you eat fish today, mister?"

"No, I don't believe I did. Why're you asking?"

"You smell like it."

He opened his jacket again. "It's the newspaper. The fish sellers on the coast wrap their fish in it when they sell it. I guess I'm so used to the smell I don't notice it anymore."

There were a lot of questions I wanted to ask this man,

but Pa had told me to hold my tongue unless spoken to. So I sat there for awhile until my curiosity got too much for me again. "Are you a bum?"

"I confess, some people have called me that."

"My pa says bums are no good. They steal from houses when the people aren't there. And the ones who don't steal come around begging all the time. My pa never gave to them, but my ma did. I saw her do it. She never told Pa."

"I see," the man said. "Did a bum ever steal from you?"

"No."

"From your pa?"

"I never heard him say so."

"Then how do you know bums steal?"

I knew it because Pa told me so. But suddenly that didn't seem like a good enough reason. "I guess I don't, really."

"Well, I'm not a bum anyway. I'm a traveling man."

"What's that?"

He shrugged. "A man who travels anywhere he wants, whenever he wants."

That sounded like the perfect life to me, picking up and going wherever you wanted without somebody saying you couldn't.

"There are three types of traveling men you'll run into," he said. "Hoboes are gentlemen who have been beaten down by life—lost everything, you might say. They ride the trains from town to town and call nowhere their home anymore. They never beg, though they aren't above asking the lady of the house if there's work to be done in exchange for a meal. Then there are the tramps who walk everywhere and look like it. They don't keep themselves up very well. They started out poor in life and that's how they'll end up. The bums are drunks and no-goods. They give traveling men a bad name. That's the sort your pa warned you against."

"Which kind are you?"

The man looked surprised. "Well, I'm a hobo, of course."

"Hoboes don't work," I said to show him I knew something about the world even if I hadn't stepped very far into it yet.

"Oh, they do sometimes. I had a job once for near a month skinning frankfurters for the Boston Sausage Co. Did a hundred pounds an hour. I was one of the fastest."

"How come you left?"

"There wasn't much room for advancement. Once you've become the fastest skinner, what's left? I decided to try my hand at dipping chocolates for Orlando Chocolate. Perhaps you've heard of them."

I looked at the man's hands wrapped in the rags. You could just see the ends of fingers sticking out here and there. "They let you dip chocolates?"

"I was cleaner then, sonny. It's mostly a woman's job, though, and didn't pay very well. Thirty cents an hour."

I let out a whistle at that. I never made thirty cents in a whole day when I helped Pa last summer.

"Thirty cents goes further when you're a boy," he said.

The man rose up and wiped the snow off his backside. I did the same. Then we walked on a little, him rustling with newspaper, me at his side. It started to feel like we were together.

"Were you always a hobo?" I said.

"No, nobody's born a hobo. I was just like you at your age. I had a home with a roof over my head and a wonderful mother."

"What happened to you?"

"I became a teacher, until fate led me in a different direction."

I didn't know what he meant by that, but I had other questions on my mind. "What do you eat?"

"Why food, of course. What do you eat?"

"I mean, how do you get food if you don't have any money?"

"Sometimes people offer it. They are very generous."

"They are? My pa told Sadie that we never give to strangers who come around. He says they should work for food like everybody else."

"That they should," the man said. "Trouble is, there are more people than jobs, so some go without. I make do with odd jobs. I'm pretty handy at fixing things for people."

"That's what my pa does, fixes things."

"An admirable profession," the man said, and then he leaned over and spit a thick brown liquid onto the snow. I looked at him closer and saw a fat wad of something stuffed in his cheek. "What's that in your mouth?"

"Chew."

"Chew?"

"Tobacco. Doesn't your pa chew?"

"I think he used to, but ma said it wasn't a proper thing to do."

"She's right. Chewing's a filthy habit. Your ma sounds like a smart woman." I wanted to say that she sure was, the smartest mother a boy could have. But I couldn't pretend she was alive, and I couldn't find the words to say she was dead, either.

"I expect she'll be wondering where you are at this time of day. You shouldn't worry your ma," the man said.

I nodded that he was right. "My quarrel isn't with her," I said, "it's with my pa."

"You two don't see eye to eye?"

That was it, sort of. "Pa and me don't see things the same way anymore."

"A young'un walks hand in hand with his pa wherever he goes. At some point you want to go a different way. You have to pull away to do it. . . . 'Two roads diverged in a wood, and I took the one less traveled by, and that has made all the difference.'"

"You took the different road?"

"That I did, just like Robert Frost said in his poem, 'The Road Not Taken.'"

Robert Frost. I knew that name from school. "He used to live in Derry. Everybody around these parts knows of him."

The man nodded. "Everybody in the country will know of him when he's dead. They'll call him a great poet."

"Why after he's dead?"

"We don't appreciate people until they're gone. That's the way it works, I'm afraid."

"Will you be appreciated when you're dead?"

He looked at me with the strangest expression, sad and puzzled at the same time. I was sorry I'd asked that.

"I hope they will," he said. "But alas, it's not everyone's fate to be remembered."

A whistle sounded far off—the evening train to Boston. We both stopped and looked back. "Seems like we have the same idea in mind," he said.

I tugged at his jacket. "Come on, then, we better hurry to the station to get our tickets."

"Tickets? A hobo doesn't pay to ride the train. He hops on."

"How does he do that?"

"My boy," the man said, "are you really wanting to go to Boston?"

"Yes sir."

"Then do as I say." He walked a few steps farther away from the station, right before the bend in the tracks. Then he knelt down, and I did the same. "The train will come by in a minute or so, and it won't have much speed yet. When it goes around the bend the conductor can't see in his mirror what's happening behind him. That's when we run for it. The door on the fifth car will open, and I'll hoist you in and then follow you. Understand?"

I couldn't believe it. Yesterday I was doing chores at

home and being yelled at by Pa like a little boy. Today I was a hobo getting ready to ride the rails!

I waited just like the man said until the front engine took the bend, then we ran up from the brush toward the train. I counted cars, and when the fifth one passed the door opened a few feet. I ran to keep up with it, and then the man lifted me under my arms toward the door. Something grabbed me that I couldn't see—it was as if the darkness had grown hands. The train sped up, and I didn't know what was happening. Where was the man? Who had he given me over to? I started toward the door to jump out, but the same hands pulled me back. A moment later I heard a thump in front of me, and then the big door slid shut. The hands let go of me, and I heard the strike of a match. A lantern lit up the car, and there was the hobo.

"You all right?" he said.

"Sure," I said, so he wouldn't think I was scared.

A voice came from behind the lantern. "Nice to see you again, Professor. Who's your traveling companion?"

The hobo crawled over toward the lantern and warmed his hands around it. "A very close friend of mine," he said. Then he turned to me. "By the way, what *is* your name?"

"Jeremy Chance" slipped from my tongue before I could stop myself. I had figured it was better nobody knew my last name, but there I had gone and blurted it out.

The hobo held out his hand. "I'm Bill Cusker. 'The Professor' some call me."

I took his hand. "Glad to meet you, 'The Professor.'"

"'Professor' is sufficient," he said. "And this is my acquaintance, the King of Ireland."

I shook the King's hand. It was very surprising, because it felt like the hand of a regular old man. "Are you really the King of Ireland?"

The man laughed. "Who's to say I'm not? How far are you going, laddie?"

"Boston," I said.

"Running away?"

It seemed to me that I wasn't really running away as much as running toward something—Davey—so I shook my head. "My brother's coming home from The War, and I'm meeting his ship."

"Anyone know you're meeting this ship?"

"Sure," I said, which wasn't a lie because I'd just told them I was, so that made two people who knew. Sometimes when it came to telling the truth or lies you had to be very careful.

"What about your pa?"

The King was getting awful particular with his questions. He wasn't giving a boy much room to move around the truth. Finally I figured that since we were on the train now and it was moving, they couldn't throw me off. So I just admitted everything. "My pa doesn't really know I'm gone. He whipped me because I said he was wrong about the fence, which he put up to spite our neighbor, Mr. Cutter, who's so old I don't really know how old, but around four score."

The King whistled. "You told your pa he was wrong?"

"Yes sir."

"About a fence?"

"It's a spite fence, which is an ugly fence you don't want to look at. He's mad because of the black walnut."

"Who's mad?"

"My pa."

"Over a black walnut?"

"Mr. Cutter has a huge black walnut on his land, and it hangs over our land and drops nuts as big as my fist. Pa wants to cut it down to build furniture on account of the woman in the Stutz Bearcat."

The Professor laughed a little. "Well, the story gets more interesting all the time."

I agreed with that. "The fancy woman drove up in this green Bearcat, it must have been twenty feet long and it was shining and sputtering, except I couldn't go outside to see it because Sadie grabbed me by the collar."

"Sadie?"

"She's my pa's cousin from down south and she hollers so loud you think your head's going to split open."

"Well, this sounds like a long story," the Professor said as he lay back on a mound of blankets, "I'm going to make myself comfortable."

The King of Ireland lay back, too, and in the warm light from the lantern, I told them everything.

BOSTON

WE PULLED INTO THE CITY late that night. It was easier getting off the train than getting on, because this time it wasn't moving.

The King of Ireland opened the sliding door a little, poked his head out, and waved the Professor to jump. Then the King put his hands under my arms like he was going to hand me out, but I squirmed free.

"I can do it myself," I said. "I jumped from my window just last week, and that's on the second floor."

"Did you now?" he said. "Then check your parachute and dive away!"

I twisted around and patted my shoulder like there was a parachute strapped to me. I gave the King the thumbs up, took a deep breath, and jumped.

The ground was farther down than I expected. I hit hard and rolled on my side, which Davey taught me to lessen the blow. The thing was, I rolled right onto the next railroad track and banged my arm. Luckily I was wearing so many clothes I didn't feel much pain.

"You all right?" the Professor said.

I hopped to my feet. "Fine as can be."

"Well then," he said as he put out his hand, "it's been a pleasure traveling with such an interesting young man."

"Yes, it was," I said as I shook with him. Then I realized that I was agreeing with him that I was an interesting young man. "You're interesting, too. I never met anybody anywheres near as interesting. You and the King."

He tipped his hat to me. The King waved at me. Then they looked about, ducked under the train, and were gone.

It happened so fast it seemed like they had melted into the dark itself. I rubbed my eyes to make sure I was seeing right. Still no Professor or King.

"Hey you, kid."

I turned behind me and saw a man near the front of the train holding a lantern. I could tell from his voice that he wasn't about to say "Welcome to Boston."

"Stay there!" he yelled, and the swinging lantern came toward me. There were trains on either side of me. I ducked down and looked under the one where the Professor and the King had gone. It was so dark I couldn't see to the other side. I sure didn't want to get stuck underneath a train. But they had gotten through that way, and they were bigger than me. Besides, the man was coming closer.

I threw myself to the ground and crawled under the train. Then I rolled. But halfway around something stopped me. I shoved myself harder, but I couldn't move. A whistle went off somewhere. What if it was this train getting ready to go back the way it had come? I'd be dragged along for miles. My body would be so torn up they probably wouldn't be able to recognize me. Pa would never know what happened to his youngest son. I'd just be gone.

The light from the lantern stopped a few feet away. I could see shoes and the bottom half of legs.

"Come on out of there," the man said.

His voice was scary. I didn't want to have to face the man who owned it. His shoe lifted up and kicked at me. He caught my shoulder, and I would have screamed except it barely hurt at all. It seemed to me that wearing two sets of clothes made a lot of sense for the kind of situations I was getting into. I wondered why I hadn't thought of it before.

I wasn't going to chance a kick to the face, so I flattened myself to the wooden ties and tried crawling rather than rolling. This time I came out on the other side.

I rose up and looked around. There was a low fence ahead of me, so I ran to it and climbed over. I felt safe now. I figured the railroad man wouldn't bother chasing a kid under a train and over a fence.

I walked up a little hill, and when I reached the top there were hundreds of lights blazing, like a sky with giant lanterns hanging in it. That had to be Boston. I'd seen pictures of it before, but never at night like this.

To be honest, the city looked exciting and frightening at the same time. I decided it would be downright foolish to go looking for Davey's ship in the dark. Besides, it wasn't due till tomorrow.

I walked a little ways and found an old shed. The door

was locked. So I sat down next to it and curled myself up. Pa used to measure the cold in dogs—how many it would take to keep you warm. With all those clothes on, this was no more than a one-dog night. I went to sleep wishing I'd brought good old Bite along with me. Then I wouldn't have been scared a bit.

———

When the sun woke me I stood up and shook myself to get the blood flowing. It was an uncommonly gentle day for January, with a bright blue sky and no more than a little of the wind that whips along the hills of Derry in winter. I wondered if it were always this nice in the city and then decided that it probably was, which is why so many people lived there.

I felt proud of myself for getting all the way to Boston without any help. Not many twelve-year-olds would be brave enough to even try it. The thing was, there wasn't anybody around to be proud in front of. Usually it was Pa who would say "Good work, boy." Sometimes Davey said, "Not bad for a little one" and then messed up my hair. If they weren't around I could always count on Bite to bark and jump on me when I did something great. Of course, I'd have to tell him the thing was great, like making that circle of snowballs around the barn window. I'd shout out, "The Amazing Jeremy T. Chance has done it again!" Bite would be on me in a second barking and licking. That dog could make any boy feel proud.

But it wasn't enough that I'd just reached Boston. I'd come to meet Davey. I figured that ships need a harbor, so all I had to do was find out where the ocean was and check out all the piers till I found the one carrying the 26th Yankee Regiment.

I shimmied up a lightpost to see over the rows of trains sitting at the station. When I got to the top, there was Boston rising up in front of my eyes, this time in the light of day. Everywhere there were buildings. Some of them looked taller than the evergreens in our back woods. Suddenly I felt awfully small.

A whistle sounded in the station, and I thought maybe I should just hop the next train heading north to Derry. The city was a dangerous place—Ma used to say that. But she thought that even Derry was dangerous, with all of its carriages and automobiles. I slid down the pole and started walking into Boston.

———

There was more to see than I ever dreamed of. I saw automobiles crawling down the road like a line of giant black beetles. I saw teams of horses pulling huge wagons full of all kinds of goods. I saw ladies with hats that looked like birds were plopped on their heads and men with long coats and canes. I saw a beggar without any legs sitting up against a wall with a little bag in his hands. A few people walking by threw pennies in it. I saw newspaper boys calling out "Prohibition Vote Tomorrow" and little

girls dressed up like dolls going into big stone churches. That seemed strange, because it was Wednesday, not Sunday.

The roads themselves were a marvel. They were paved shiny black. Whatever the black stuff was felt kind of hard and soft at the same time under my boots. Pa had told us there was a mile of road over in Hooksett paved this way. I could see why the automobiles would like it better than dirt, but it seemed unnatural to make horses trot on such a thing. I bet Licker wouldn't set a hoof on it without bucking up.

I walked down streets so narrow I could almost reach out and touch the buildings on both sides. The air was filled with the smell of baked breads and roasting coffee. Signs on the stores said *panettiere* and *caffettiere*. It seemed like I was in a foreign country, and I began to wonder if the Professor had been fooling me and this were some other place than Boston.

When you don't know something, ask—that's what my ma used to say. So I stopped outside a shop with beautiful white cakes in the window. Every time somebody went in or out I breathed in the sweetness. After doing that for a while I got up my nerve to step in front of an old man bent half over. He reminded me of Cutter.

"Excuse me, sir, is this Boston?"

"Si, si."

I didn't know what he said, but he was nodding at the same time, which meant "yes." Then he smiled at me, and I could see his mouth had only one or two teeth in it. I wondered how he ate meat like that. Thinking of meat made me think of another question.

"Do you know where I can get something to eat that doesn't cost very much?"

"Si, si," he said again and pointed over my shoulder. "Around the corner from Scollay Square. Joe and Nemo." With that he was gone.

I started walking the way he pointed, and there was a roar above me. I looked up at a huge steel *something* over my head. I thought about this steel thing for a moment, but thinking didn't get me any closer to understanding what was going on up there. So I stopped the next person who came by, a man walking a large shaggy gray dog about twice as big as Bite.

"Excuse me, mister, what's up there?"

The man leaned his head back. The dog looked up, too. "The sky?"

"Below the sky, on top of the steel thing."

"It's the El, kid."

"The *L?*"

"The Atlantic Elevated train line. It just went up a few years ago."

Imagine . . . a train that ran on tracks up in the air. Sadie wouldn't believe it.

I walked a block until I came to a wide open street with the letters SCOLLAY SQ running from top to bottom on a building. There was more happening in this square than all of Derry. The noise of people and automobiles was so loud I almost couldn't hear myself think. So I just

walked and looked until I found myself in front of the
most interesting place I'd ever seen: the Old Howard
Theater. The sign on the window said, "Always Something
Doing, One to Eleven, at the Old Howard." Just below
that another sign said, "25 Beautiful Girls 25!" I was sure
curious what twenty-five beautiful girls were doing inside
this place, but the giant clock on top of the PM Scotch
billboard at the end of the square said half past eleven.
The theater wouldn't open for more than an hour, which
was good, because I had to save my money for food.

I turned away from the Old Howard and looked across
Scollay Square. Up a side street I could see "Joe and
Nemo," just like the old man had told me. The problem
was that between it and me were all sorts of automobiles
and horses and wagons and people. I could figure only
one way to get across: I put my head down and ran. I
heard horns honking and men yelling and tires screeching
and horses clomping past me. I didn't stop for anything.
I zigged and zagged and finally made it to the other side,
right in front of this place called "Joe and Nemo."

I'd never eaten in a restaurant before, and I didn't
know how to do it. But I was so hungry I figured this was
the time to learn.

I waited till the door opened and two men came out.
Before the door closed I scooted in.

"Can I help you?" a woman asked me.

"A man told me I could eat here."

"Well, he was right about that."

"He said it doesn't cost a lot."

"Right again. You can't beat Joe and Nemo's prices. You want to sit at a table?"

"Does that cost more?"

The woman leaned against the counter. "I can see you're on a tight budget, so why don't you tell me how much money you have exactly, and I'll tell you what you can afford?"

I pulled my fist full of coins from my pocket and laid everything on the counter. She spread apart my pennies and nickels in order to count them.

"Exactly two bits—that will get you a nice big bowl of beef stew and a glass of milk. How does that sound?"

"I'm not partial to milk. Coffee would suit me."

"Then stew and coffee it is. You sit at the end of the counter here, and I'll get your order."

She went through swinging doors and came back out faster than I could do anything except take off my outermost jacket and lay it across my legs. She set a big bowl of stew in front of me. It was so thick that the spoon was standing straight up in the middle of it. On the plate was a hunk of black bread. I grabbed the bread and ate it in three bites. Then I started in on the stew.

"Where's the fire?" the woman said.

I turned around but didn't see anything outside. "There's a fire?"

"I meant how come you're eating so fast? We don't charge by the minute."

"Oh, okay."

"You're not from the city, are you?"

"I'm from Derry. That's north of here in a whole different state. I came to meet my brother. A ship's bringing him home from The War today. Do you know which way the harbor is?"

"Just take a right outside the door and follow your nose to Commercial Street. Go too far and you'll fall in the ocean."

She left to tend to other customers, and I felt proud of myself again. Here I was eating in a restaurant by myself. I couldn't wait to see what other adventures were waiting for me in this city.

I finished the stew and stacked my coins on the counter. I figured I shouldn't just leave them there where somebody might snatch them, so I waited. In a minute the woman came through the swinging doors carrying a piece of pie. It smelled like apple. There was a scoop of vanilla ice cream sitting on top. I was wondering who was getting to eat pie at this time of day when she set the plate down in front of me. "It's on the house," she said.

"Excuse me?"

"It's free."

"Pie's free in Boston?"

She laughed at me, but not a mean laugh. "No, just today apple pie is free to boys from Derry, New Hampshire, who don't have the money to pay for it."

"That's me," I said and dug my fork into the thick gooey crust. Pie never tasted so good.

EXPLOSION

MY NEXT ADVENTURE came sooner than I expected.

It started with the rum balls, which were sitting on a shelf outside a market called Sulley's. There were Black Jack licorice strips and caramels on the shelf, too, but I was only interested in the rum balls.

The sign said, "RUM BALLS—1 Cent Ea." That seemed like a bargain to me. But when I reached into my pocket, my hand came out empty. I knew I'd only brought with me the twenty-five cents, exactly what I'd spent at Joe and Nemo's. I'd counted my money a dozen times before I left Derry. But still I was hoping that maybe I'd counted wrong all those times and what I'd really had was twenty-six cents. That would mean one penny was still stuck in my pocket. I stuffed my hand in again and wiggled my fingers around. They felt nothing.

On just one meal I'd spent all that I'd saved in six months. Pa would say I didn't know the value of money, but he'd be wrong again. Right then I did know the exact value of money. One cent equaled one rum ball.

I turned to leave, but my feet didn't move. I turned back to the rum balls. They looked awful good. The sinful thought ran through my head, why not just take one?

Ma said the city was Satan's backyard. If that was true, then candy was the devil's bait for a boy. I could hear the devil's voice in my head: *Taking one little rum ball doesn't make you a thief. It's like picking an apple off your neighbor's tree when he has so many of them.*

It *was* like that. Every afternoon in the fall I'd pick an apple off of one of Simpson's trees on my way home from school. He had hundreds of apples hanging from hundreds of trees. He sure wouldn't miss my one little apple each day.

I knew stealing things was wrong—I learned that from Pa. But I didn't know for myself it was wrong. What I mean is, since I never tried stealing, I didn't know exactly what was wrong with it. Besides, this seemed more like taking than stealing.

I figured that growing up was the time to try out all sorts of things. Like cussing, for instance. If I tried all the cusses on for size when I was young, then when I grew up I'd know right off which one was fit to use for what occasion. Except Pa heard me behind the woodshed practicing "damnation" and "son of a worm-eating dog," meaning The Kaiser, who was the leader of Germany. I tried explaining how I wasn't cursing for real, I was just practicing for when I grew up. Pa just raised his hand to me saying if he heard another cuss out of me I wouldn't have any growing up to practice for.

But I remembered something else Pa said, "Never let Opportunity pass you by." Rum balls sitting without an eye on them sure seemed like Opportunity to me.

There was Ma to consider, too, though. The last thing she said to me was, "I'll be watching you from heaven, Jeremy." I didn't really think she was sitting up there in heaven with some sort of giant eyeglass that could see every little thing I did. Still, she did say she would be watching. I'd have to be sneaky about it.

I stood on my toes like I was looking at a sailor climbing the cat's walk on the big ship in the harbor. Then I backed up to the candy counter whistling "Three Blind Mice," as casual as could be. A man wearing an apron was just inside the door stacking cans. I whistled, backed up a foot, then snitched a handful of rum balls into my trouser pocket.

The fright skittered through me like I had touched electricity. I thought for sure that Sulley himself was going to bust through his door and grab me. Stealing wasn't as much fun as I had thought.

I decided to put the rum balls back just as I had taken them, without being seen. But all of a sudden everything started shaking and growling. I figured I'd gone and started something dreadful for sure. When an honest boy steals rum balls, the One Who Made Us couldn't be pleased.

I looked around to make sure the rumbling wasn't just some crazy idea that got into my head. Sometimes I imagined war all about Derry, and me a doughboy shooting it out with the Gerries. But this noise was real all right.

People were jumping back and forth in different directions on the street, nobody knowing what was coming from which way. The old men sitting on the benches up in the park were shuffling away and bumping into each other. It was kind of funny, if you could see the humor of the situation.

Then there was a loud popping in the air, like bombs going off, and the wind picked up worse than a blow at sea. I turned circles every which way trying to see, but that just made me dizzy.

I was a true American boy, ready on the watch when President Wilson told everybody to keep their eyes out for Germans invading us by the coast. But I wasn't ready for what happened next. A whip of wind snuck up behind me and lifted me off my feet like I was a slip of rum ball wrapper. It blew me through the air just as if I'd grown wings, then dropped me back on the ground. Now I knew how geese felt getting pelted out of the sky by Pa's long rifle.

I looked over my arms and legs. I still had two of each in the right places. When I looked up again, I couldn't believe what my eyes were telling me—a wave as tall as a battleship was rolling down Commercial Street. Now the real uncommon thing was that this wave was thick black, not like any I saw when Pa took us to the Atlantic.

Well, being scared from stealing was one thing. But being scared from looking at something huge coming at you that's tossing trucks upside down like they were toys and not knowing what this wave was, that downright scared the spit from me. I stuttered the fastest prayer God ever heard, and the most truthful, too.

I closed my eyes hoping that maybe I was dreaming and I'd wake up and laugh at how I'd scared myself over nothing. But when this mysterious wave hit me I knew it wasn't any dream. It was molasses.

It was hot and thick as . . . well, thick as blackstrap molasses that you put in hotcakes and cookies. This molasses broke over my head and flipped me around till I didn't know which way was sky. The molasses was too heavy for me to lift free my hands, so there was only one thing left to do—eat my way to the top! I gulped and swallowed and gulped some more. I must have taken in a gallon of molasses before I suddenly got tossed above the wave and could breathe again. My face was burning a little and I tried wiping it clear, but there was no part of my arm clean enough to do the wiping. I shook my head like Bite does after a dip in the lake, then opened one eye.

It was an amazing sight—the world suddenly covered with molasses, just like a blanket of brown snow. To the left of me was the fire company building where I'd just waved to the men inside. It was folded up like a house of cards knocked over by someone's hand. Sulley's Market was gone.

I could barely unstick myself from the pavement to stand up. The molasses was flowing past me now on either side of my legs. For a moment it was as quiet as midnight in Derry.

"What in the world?" a man called out from behind me.

Another man answered him, "It's molasses. I'll be a drowned dog if it ain't molasses."

I could have told him as much. If you're standing up to your knees in something, you should be able to tell what it is.

Slowly the molasses flowed on by until it was no deeper than a creek you step into to cool your feet on a summer day. Except this molasses was warm. Voices were yelling on top of each other.

"Hold the horse, rein him in . . ."

"This way, give a hand . . ."

"It was the old Purity Distilling. The tank exploded . . ."

"Why, there were two million gallons of molasses in there . . ."

"Maria, has anyone seen my little girl, Maria? . . ."

"Just like a volcano it erupted . . ."

"There, under the wagon, look . . . Oh God, no!"

Something important was happening just ahead of me. Men as dark as coal miners were pulling something from under an ice wagon. It was a little girl, and she hung over a man's arms like a dead dog I picked up in the road once.

"Got to get her to the hospital, hurry."

Sirens were blaring from every side of the city. I turned about and couldn't believe my eyes again. I was staring at a house. Now I knew that me and the house weren't neighbors a minute ago, but I couldn't be sure which of us moved where.

I couldn't be sure of much, what with everything soaked brown like it had been dipped in a trough of chocolate. I couldn't wait to tell Davey about this. I bet he never saw such destruction even in The War.

It was strange the way something as ordinary as molasses could turn mean and killing if there were enough of it. I guess a thirty-foot wave of most anything would cause its problems. Like manure, for instance, or even milk. I couldn't abide even the smell of milk up close, so I'd surely be dead if a tank full of that exploded on me.

There was more going on around me than I could sort out with just one clear eye. So I reached under my jackets and found a dry spot on my shirt to rub off my face.

Hundreds of Johnny-come-latelies were dashing about now. You could tell them apart because they were clean white except for their shoes.

A hand shook my shoulder. It was a reverend all dressed up in black like he'd just run from church. "You okay, son?"

"Yes sir," I answered as he took the arm of his sleeve and wiped around my ears. "I'm as fine as can be expected."

"Were you with anyone, anyone to look for?"

"No sir, I'm all there is here."

A scream nearby was fit to chill your teeth. The reverend patted me on the back and took off toward the sound. I ran after him, hopping over all sorts of objects covered with molasses. Suddenly he stopped under the elevated railroad tracks, and I plowed right into him, knocking him face down into the molasses. He picked himself up and looked at me like he wanted to cuss me, but of course, being a reverend, he couldn't.

We found the noise—it was a woman sitting next to one of the supports that held up the elevated. She was holding her head, and I figured the molasses had thrown her into the steel column. I looked up, and the beam above us was twisted out a little. It seemed to me that it might collapse any second. The reverend saw it, too. But still he knelt down by the woman and comforted her and said he wouldn't leave her.

A scream from behind scared me so much I jumped and almost knocked over the reverend again. I figured I was of better use elsewhere and took off running. But the sound of bullets stopped me cold—not cold dead, just cold surprised.

"Public Works, North End Paving Division," read the sign above the stable doors that stood wide open. Inside, molasses filled the stalls. I stepped to the door, looked in, and there was a sight to make me sicker than any dog.

Horses were stuck up to their bellies in molasses. They whined a sorrowful noise. The wave had trapped a dozen of them against the back wall, crippling and tangling their legs. A man was wading from stall to stall, waist high in molasses. He patted each horse's head, gentle like, then raised his pistol. I hated watching an animal die like that, but I knew it was better than their suffering.

If someone had rolled up a coffin right then, I'd have jumped in. That's how sick I felt from gulping molasses and seeing horses die. Everything I ate that day took the opportunity to throw up at my feet, and not a little of it was brown molasses.

I turned away for air. There were hundreds of people now coming to see what the molasses had done. On the other side of the street, a truck pulled up and a dozen policemen jumped out. When I looked to the harbor I saw two lines of jackies from the ship running double quick to help. As they came closer I could hear their munitions belts rattling about their waists. I started over to see the sailors up close when a bluecoat nabbed me by the collar.

"Whoa there, sonny," he said. "Where you heading so lickety-split?"

It took me some time to figure out his meaning 'cause like Pa said, folks in Boston spoke English differently from us normal folk.

"Nowheres in particular," I said. "I'm just seeing all that's happening."

"Someone looking after you?"

"I got a brother over there," I said pointing toward the ships. "He'll be coming for me soon," I added, so the policeman didn't think I was alone.

"Why don't you make it easy on him to find you," he said, "and stay behind the lines now?"

I stood there for a moment under the officer's eye, but there was too much to see to stand still. After all, I'd been in the middle of the explosion and not gotten hurt. What could happen to me now?

The policemen were holding hands in a row to keep people back. I fell to my knees and crawled past their legs. It was easy for one as small as myself to scoot by them in all of the commotion and make off into the molasses again.

The first thing I heard while running down Commercial Street was someone calling as polite as can be, "Oh young man, excuse me." It sounded like a voice coming from another house that had no business sitting in the middle of the street.

"Yoo-hoo, up here."

I looked up, and there was a little hand waving a white handkerchief from the dormer window. "What can I do for you, ma'am?"

"Well," she said, "I believe my sister and I need assistance coming down from here."

That seemed odd to me. "Why don't you just walk down your stairs and out the front door?"

"We're a bit weary from the excitement, you understand, and I'm not sure there are any stairs left. Would you be so kind as to call someone in authority?"

I turned on my heels and stuck two fingers in my mouth for a ripping whistle, even with the molasses sticking to my hand. When a sailor came running over, I pointed to the old lady and was on my way again.

I ran back to the firehouse, Engine Company 31. The firemen had stripped off their jackets and were swinging sledge hammers into the rubble. Their arms were thick and copper colored, coated with molasses. They pounded clear a little opening, and the fire chief bent over to look in. I wondered what was inside to see.

"We'll need the torch," he yelled. "There's a chunk of steel wedged in here."

A fireman no older than Davey set the torch on fire.

Sparks flew ten feet as he burned a hole bigger and bigger until the chief could reach his hand through.

"Keep going," he said, "fast as you can.

I watched the hole opening wider and wider and I said to myself, "I bet I could squeeze through there." Except I must have said this out loud. A fireman lifted me up by one arm and carried me to the front.

"This boy says he could crawl through the hole, chief. He could make it in and tell us if Gallagher's dead or alive."

The chief looked at me from tip to toe. "You think you could get through there?" he asked.

"I've crawled through smaller spaces before. Like one time . . ."

"The building's done all the falling it's going to, I'd say. Still, you never know. What's your name?"

"Jeremy T. Chance. The T stands for Trouble, my Pa says, but it's really Theopoulos."

A few of the men laughed at that.

"He around here, your pa?"

"No, I'm on my own."

"Okay, Trouble," the chief said to me, "let's see if you can get through that hole and find Gallagher."

I took off my coats and pulled one sweater and then the other off me, then one of my shirts. After that I took off my boots and yanked off my extra pair of pants.

"You always wear this much?" the chief asked.

"Just today," I said.

"Lucky you did. All of those clothes may have saved you from getting burned by the molasses."

I went up to the hole and stuck one arm and one shoulder through, then the other arm and shoulder. That's the trick of squeezing through a small place. After that it was easy. I grabbed onto something solid inside and pulled myself into the rubble. I could hear the firemen on the other side cheering.

I'd never seen such confusion before. Everything had fallen down. There were desks knocked over and chairs broken. The ceiling was bending low. The air was fuming dust from the bricks split open. And of course there was molasses sticking to everything.

I stopped at the fireman's pole and figured that was a good way to see around. I leaped up as far as I could and grabbed on, but my hands were so slippery with molasses I slid down right away. I walked around a little and called out "Gallagher," then listened. I heard nothing. I explored some more, pulling away pieces of wood as I went, and then stepped on something soft. I leaned over to see what it was and about jumped out of my one remaining trousers. It was a stomach! I pulled away some more wood, and there was the head to go with the stomach of Gallagher.

"You okay, mister?"

He didn't answer except to moan and point at his leg. I looked down, and he sure had something to complain about. There was a whole piano collapsed on the lower part of his body! I put my shoulder to it, but my little weight couldn't move it an inch.

Pa taught me that what you couldn't do with your arms you should try with your head, and this seemed to fit the situation perfectly. I sat down next to Gallagher in the molasses. Maybe he thought I was fooling around because thinking can look like fooling. I tried remembering if there was any other situation like this I ever heard of and something popped into my mind. It was a couple of years ago when the hurricane blew up the coast. That storm knocked over half a dozen trees around our house. One of them was the big beech, and it was too heavy for us to move from across the front path. So Pa set up a lever with a smaller branch and stuck that under the beech. Then he found a round piece of wood to wedge under the lever—that was the fulcrum, he said. He put his weight to one end of the lever and suddenly the other end lifted the beech tree a few feet. When I asked him how he did it, he said it was Science. He said you could move the world with a big enough lever.

I didn't need to move the world, just a piano. I looked around and saw a piece of wood as tall as Pa that could make the lever. I figured I could use the piano stool for the fulcrum. It took some maneuvering, but I was able to push down on the length of wood resting on the stool, and darned if that piano didn't raise up a little off the man's leg.

"Can you move, Mr. Gallagher?"

He nodded and slid himself free. When he was clear I let the piano bang back to the floor.

Gallagher sat up and looked at me with an expression I hadn't seen very often.

"You're one smart boy, aren't you?"

I didn't know how to answer that. You're not supposed

to call yourself smart. "It's just something I learned from my pa," I said. "He knows everything."

Gallagher couldn't stand up, but he could crawl, and I helped by pulling on his belt. By the time we made it back to the hole, it was wide enough for a man to get through. Hands reached in from the outside and pulled him out. Then they reached in for me, too. I stepped backward a little, because it was interesting being inside this rubble. I figured I'd never get a place like this to myself again. I didn't want to leave yet.

The chief stuck his head through the hole. "Come on, Trouble, you have to get out of there."

"I could look around for more people," I said.

"Everyone else is accounted for."

I turned around for one last look. "There could be some animals. Didn't you have a dog in this firehouse?"

"No, we didn't. You mind me, Trouble, and come out."

So I crawled back through the hole and out into the light.

HERO

NO ONE HAD EVER CHEERED for me before, but they were sure cheering now. The firemen passed me down the line like I was a log and patted my head. Sailors were clapping and policemen pointing at me and just regular people were smiling and yelling.

The chief lifted me onto his shoulder, and I could see over everybody's heads, which was strange for a twelve-year-old.

"This boy," he said and reached his hand up to take mine, "performed the work of a grown man today. And he did it like a hero not thinking of his own safety. That's the spirit that won us a war."

The people whooped it up and stomped their feet.

"Now let's get to work cleaning up this city."

The chief set me on the ground again, and suddenly it was over. The firemen moved off in different directions. I didn't know which way to go. A policeman took me by the collar. "Come on, Trouble," he said, "let's get you cleaned up."

I took a few steps with him, and the crowd parted, like

it was Teddy Roosevelt himself coming through. Then standing right in front of me was something more surprising than any molasses explosion: Pa!

"Jeremy Chance," he said in the voice he used whenever I got into a situation, "what trouble did you get into this time?"

He reached for me, but the policeman pushed his hand away. "Hold on now, who would you be?"

"I'd be his pa."

"That so, Trouble?"

For a moment—just the smallest, tiniest bit of a moment—I thought about saying, "Never saw him before in my life." Then I could run off and find Davey, and who knows what would happen next? The city had turned out to be a very unpredictable place.

"Jeremy," he said, "speak up."

"He's Pa," I said.

The policeman broke out into a big smile and shoved me forward. "Well then, mister, you must be very proud of a boy like this."

"Proud? Isn't he in some trouble?"

"Not today he isn't. Didn't you hear?"

Pa shook his head. "I just now saw the crowd and came over. I've been looking for him all morning."

"Well, he's a hero. That's what the fire chief called him. Saved a man's life."

"A hero?" Pa said, like the policeman had just said I was a boy from Mars or somewhere even farther out in the sky.

"That's right."

"He's a hero?" Pa said again, like maybe he was confused by the accent.

This was getting kind of embarrassing. Of course I'd never been a hero before, so I could see how he wasn't expecting it. But there was a first time for everything.

"You can take him over to the Red Cross tent," the policeman said. "Get him cleaned off before that molasses sticks to him permanently."

Pa led me off to the Red Cross ladies who gave us a bucket of water. He made me strip off my remaining trousers and shirt right there with the women around. I was shivering until he started swabbing me with warm water.

"I don't understand any of this," he said as he took a rag to my arms.

I think it was the first time I ever heard him admit that. Maybe it was being in the city that was confusing him, because back home in Derry Pa knew everything.

"It was the molasses tank," I said. "Purity Distilling. It exploded over everything, including me. It blew me into the air and all of a sudden I was leaning against a house which wasn't next to me before, and they shot the horses, Pa, it was terrible, and the lady with the handkerchief called to me from the second story—that was after I knocked over the reverend, he was holding the woman's hand under the elevated with the train hanging over the side. Oh, yeah, and the girl died under the ice wagon."

"Well," Pa said after a minute, "I guess that makes everything clear as mud."

I laughed because I knew he was joking with me, even though he wasn't smiling. Pa could joke with a serious face.

"So all that makes you a hero?"

"No, that was afterward at the firehouse. It fell down, and Gallagher was trapped inside. I offered myself to crawl through the hole to find him. It was spooky, Pa, and I stepped on his stomach. His legs were caught under a piano."

"You pulled him out from under a piano?"

"No, he rolled out on his own after I lifted the piano."

"You lifted a whole piano?"

"Sure, Pa, me and the lever. Remember, you taught me how when we were trying to move the beech tree after the hurricane?"

Pa stepped back and looked at me. "I remember, but I didn't think you were listening."

"Sure I was listening."

He went back to rubbing my arms with the rag. "This molasses is dried on you like a second skin. Cousin Sadie will have to take the horse brush to you." He folded his arms. "That is, if you're planning to come home."

I didn't understand. Of course I was coming home. I didn't have a choice, did I?

"If a boy's old enough to be a hero," he said, "I suppose he's old enough to decide if he needs a pa looking after him anymore. Isn't that right?"

"I guess," I said, because I didn't want to go against what he was saying. But the truth was standing there half naked, covered in molasses, I did feel the need to have someone looking after me. The world was a lot more dangerous than I'd thought.

"I'm not really a hero, Pa. I mean, I sort of was for a few minutes, but I'm back to being a regular boy now."

"A regular boy who walks away from the house and hops a train with a strange man?"

"That was the Professor. He isn't really strange. He can quote poetry."

"Can he now? So while he's quoting poetry to you, your pa is tracking you into Derry and onto the Boston train and into the middle of a molasses flood?"

That seemed like a miracle to me. "How *did* you track me so fast?"

"You never have been good at sneaking. A dozen people saw you, including the stationmaster in Boston. Said you ran under the train."

"It wasn't moving, Pa."

"I know that, Jeremy," he said like I'd just come out with the stupidest statement a boy ever made.

"But then in the whole big city you found me."

"There was no miracle to finding you. You're my son, and I know you. I figured you'd be looking for Davey's ship, so I was heading to the harbor. Then I heard the explosion and saw all the commotion around the firehouse. That seemed like the place to look for you."

While Pa was explaining how he found me he was wringing the molasses out of my clothes. When he twisted my trousers, his hand felt something in my pocket. "What do you have in here?"

"Nothing," I said.

He reached inside and pulled out a sticky mass of rum balls.

"What are these?"

"I think I need some more water," I said as I rubbed my legs.

"I asked you what these are, Jeremy."

"I suppose they're the rum balls."

"Where'd you get rum balls?"

"From Sulley's. That's a market."

"You had money to waste on buying candy?"

"Well . . ." The truth was I didn't waste my money on rum balls at all. I'd bought a whole meal of beef stew with my two bits. It seemed to me that he would hate stealing a lot more than wasting. But I couldn't lie, not to the one who'd come all the way from Derry looking for me.

"I didn't exactly spend my money on them, Pa. My hand kind of just sort of picked them up and then there was the explosion."

"You were meaning to pay for them?"

I would have, if I'd had the money. But I wasn't meaning to pay. "No, Pa."

I figured I was in for a licking, and maybe he'd do it right there in front of the Red Cross ladies in the nice gray dresses. But he just shook his head at me.

"You did a man's job today saving that fireman," he said,

"so you're too old to feel my belt on you anymore. I'll just say this: I thank the Lord you're alive, but I'm disappointed a son of mine would steal."

Those words hurt me more than any whipping. I wanted to say to him, "Please, Pa, I'm not too old for a licking, really!" But he was already walking away toward the harbor. We were going to find Davey.

DAVEY!

A BIG GRAY SHIP as long as a whole train of coal cars
stretched out into the harbor. Four white smokestacks
taller than steeples on a church were sticking up in the
middle. It seemed to me a marvel that something as big
as a ship could float. When I threw a stone into the pond
out back, it sank straight away. Yet this ship, which was
millions of times heavier, was sitting nice and easy on
the water.

I thought to ask Pa about this, but at that moment two
sailors appeared on the back deck and started lowering
a gangplank. There were hundreds of us waiting on the
dock, and everyone cheered. I cheered and whistled, too.
If Davey was in earshot, he'd know it was me. He said I
could whistle louder than a train.

"Come on, Jeremy," Pa said and yanked me almost off
my feet. We hurried with everyone else toward the rear.
When we got there soldiers were already running down the
gangplank. They had wide-brimmed hats on and trousers
that came just below the knee, like baseball players wore.

When they got to the deck it was if they were swallowed up by the crowd. Everyone was hugging and kissing and cheering some more. I couldn't wait to see my brother. I figured he'd pick me up and throw me over his shoulder like he did at home. I used to kick and scream about it, especially when he spun me around until I was dizzy between the ears. But when Davey went off to The War, that was one of the things I missed.

"Where is he, Pa?"

"He'll be coming."

"But he should have been first off. You know he always likes being first."

"The army doesn't run according to what a person likes, Jeremy. He has to wait his turn."

Pa went up on his toes, and I wondered what he could see that I couldn't. I wished he would raise me onto his shoulders like he used to do so I could get a better look, but a boy my age couldn't ask for that. So I stretched up on my own toes. I still couldn't see past Pa's shoulder.

"Let's move down a little farther," he said. We pushed past some people until we were only a few yards from the end of the gangplank. We watched there for a maddening amount of time until the stream of soldiers turned into a trickle. Then none at all. Everyone else on the pier was gone. After awhile the two sailors in white uniforms appeared on deck again and hauled the gangplank on board.

"Pa, where is he? They're done getting off."

"I can see that, Jeremy. Just hold on."

He cupped his hands around his mouth and called up

to the sailors. "Can you tell me, did all those from the Yankee 26th get off?"

One of the sailors nodded and then ducked inside a door. Pa turned around. He scratched his head. I didn't like seeing that because it meant he didn't know what was going on any better than me. Then a thought worse than any other I could imagine came to me—Davey was dead. The Influenza could have taken him, too, right after he sent his last letter, maybe even while he was on the ship. Or maybe the infection did him in. There wouldn't have been any way for the army to send us the notification. It was the only answer that made sense—Davey was dead.

"Come on," Pa said. "Let's see if we can't find somebody in charge."

I didn't move. Asking somebody wouldn't make any difference. Dead was dead.

"Jeremy?"

"I think he's gone, Pa."

He stared down on me with a fierce look. "He's not gone, he's just missing for a minute."

"I feel it, Pa. I stole rum balls and angered God, that's why he sent the molasses, and maybe he took Davey, too."

"Hold on now, boy, you're running all sorts of things together that are separate."

They didn't seem separate to me. "God punishes the wicked, doesn't he? Cousin Sadie says that all the time."

"Well, yes, but—"

"And I was wicked for stealing."

"You were wrong for stealing, Jeremy, not wicked.

And the tank probably burst because the molasses fermented. You remember when Shaw's silo full of fermenting corn exploded, don't you?"

"Yes."

"Well that's what happened here, I'll bet."

"But—"

"No more *buts*, Jeremy. Now let's look for Davey."

We turned to go, but I kept looking back at the ship in case they put the gangplank back out for Davey to get off. I didn't know where we were going, and I didn't ask.

———————

We walked up one street and down another. Pa seemed to choose which way we went by how much molasses we had to step through. The smell of it was as strong as if I'd just stuck my nose in a bottle of it. Some folks were shoveling the sidewalks of the molasses and others were trying to wash it away with buckets of water.

Pa shook his head and said, "They might get rid of the sight of molasses, but the smell will hang on things around here for years."

That smell was making me powerful hungry for cake or biscuits, anything that would stick to your ribs. I figured that when I threw up the molasses, Joe and Nemo's beef stew had come with it. So my stomach was empty. But I couldn't ask Pa to spend money at a restaurant, even one that didn't cost much. Besides, I shouldn't have been thinking of eating when we were looking for Davey.

We turned left and right and left and left again. I sure hoped Pa was paying attention, because I was surely lost. Every time he saw a soldier he asked, "Are you from the Yankee 26th? You know Davey Chance?" Nobody did.

"I expect he didn't make that ship," Pa said. "He'll be on the next one."

"But the next one might not be for a month."

"Then that's when we'll see him, in a month. We might as well find our way back to the train station."

"No, Pa, we haven't looked enough. We—"

A door opened in front of us, and a half-dozen soldiers stumbled out. I could hear a song coming from inside, and the tune was familiar, "What a Friend We Have in Jesus." That hymn was one of my ma's favorites. But the words weren't anything like I heard in church.

When this lousy war is over,
no more soldiering for me,
When I get my civvy clothes on,
oh how happy I shall be.

I looked up at the sign overhead, "The Atlantic Tavern." The door shut, stopping the song. I turned to Pa, but he was halfway across the street, following one of the soldiers that had split off from the rest. I figured he was going to ask about my brother. But as I ran up to Pa I heard him call out, "Davey?"

The soldier whirled around, and I vow I could have been knocked over by a feather. It *was* him!

"Pa? Jeremy?" He dropped his bag in the middle of the street and ran toward us. We grabbed each other and hugged, just like the people on the dock.

Then he pulled away and said, "What are you doing here? I didn't expect you'd be coming all the way to Boston to meet me."

"It was kind of unexpected," Pa said and twirled the side of his mustache, which was a habit of his. Davey twirled the right side of *his* mustache, which he never had before. I reached up and rubbed above my lip. There was nothing to twirl.

"We were looking for you all over," I said. "You didn't come off the ship, and I thought you were dead but Pa said you weren't."

"They let some of us off earlier this morning, Jeremy, and I went out with the boys for a b—." Davey looked over my head at Pa.

"What's a b—?" I asked.

"He means a beer," Pa said.

My brother nodded. "It was like a farewell drink. I only had one."

"It's your business if you have a beer or not," Pa said. "A man who fights in a war makes his own choices."

"Yes sir. But I don't think I'll be drinking again any time soon. The taste is awful bitter."

"That's for the better. I read that Nebraska is likely to vote in Prohibition tomorrow. That's the last state that's needed. It's a crazy thing when the government can tell you what you can drink and not drink."

"Some of the boys are going to drink all night," Davey said.

"They'll be throwing up all morning," Pa said. "Then they'll be wishing Prohibition had started one day sooner." With that he twirled his mustache again, and Davey did, too. I had never noticed before how much he and Pa looked alike.

Davey rubbed his right arm with his left hand.

"How is that?" Pa said.

"It's still kind of sore, but it's getting better every day. The infection's gone."

"You go easy on it. It will mend faster."

"I'll carry your bag," I said and ran back for it. But I could barely lift it off the ground a foot. That was embarrassing.

Davey came up behind me, grabbed the handles, and swung the bag over his good left shoulder. "Most boys your age couldn't budge that at all," he said. "You've gotten stronger."

I didn't really feel much stronger, but if Davey said so, I figured it must be so.

Our train home didn't reach Derry till after dark. This time I left by the steps, which wasn't anywhere near as exciting as jumping out like I did with the Professor and the King.

Davey said he had money enough to hire Sam Barnes

to take us out to our place in his wagon. Sam was always ready to drive folks around who needed a ride, no matter the hour.

"As long as we have legs, we might as well use them," Pa said as the train pulled out of the station. "That money can be put to better purpose." He winked at me then, and I figured he meant the new house he was planning to build us.

"What purpose did you have in mind?" Davey asked.

I looked at Pa. I was bursting to tell.

"Go ahead, boy, before you bust open a gut holding it in."

"We're getting a new house, Davey! Pa's going to build it for us, and it's going to have the outhouse inside like they do some places in Derry and a proper tub to wash in and it will have ten rooms and . . ."

"Hold on, now, Jeremy, I didn't say I'd be building a mansion."

"Maybe eight rooms," I said. "That would be enough."

Davey adjusted the bag on his shoulder. "No more raining on us in the middle of the night, right, brother?"

"Right, brother," I said.

"Now let's get us on home to the *old* house," Pa said. "Sadie's probably worried sick about us."

So we set off. Pa could walk near as fast as a horse could trot. But for the first time I ever saw, Davey was matching him, stride for stride, even carrying his big bag. Me, I had to run a little every so often just to keep up with them.

"You should have seen Derry when news came that The War was over, Davey. They let us out of school. Everybody was in the streets making noise and shouting, 'The War's over. We won!'"

Pa stopped quick, and I did, too. "Nobody really wins a war," he said. "Just some people lose less than others. In this war we were favored that the fighting was across the Atlantic and not on our own soil."

We walked on some more, past the Curley place where every room seemed lit up. That was almost a mansion, except it wasn't fancy like the ones I'd seen in magazines. The Curley house was just big, which it had to be to fit all of those children. Something swooped over the road ahead of us—a crow, I think—and Davey pointed at it.

"I saw something at the front you won't believe," he said.

"What's that, Davey?"

"The German bombs kept blowing up our telephone wires, so the fastest way to get word from headquarters up to the trenches was by pigeon."

I was expecting him to say by horse or dog or maybe even a trained rabbit. But . . . a pigeon?

"That's right. We had one called Gunpowder who carried messages back and forth for us. We wouldn't have known when to advance or retreat or which way to move without that bird. A lot of animals helped us, like horses and mules. They pulled our guns and supplies all the way across France."

"What was it like?" I said, "being in The War, I mean."

He laughed a little. "Seemed like it was digging more than anything."

"Digging?"

"Every time we advanced another mile or so, we stopped and dug ourselves trenches to lie in for the night. That could take hours. Sometimes we could hear the Boche digging their own trenches."

"The Boche?"

"That's what we called the Germans."

"You mean they were so close you could hear them?"

Davey nodded. "A couple of our boys knew German and called out to them. They talked back and forth for hours."

"It's a strange war," Pa said, "where the enemies talk to each other in the dark and then shoot each other when light comes."

"They were just like us," Davey said, "farm boys who wished to be home with their families."

"What did it feel like getting shot, Davey?"

"Felt like somebody took a hot poker from the fire and jabbed it in my shoulder, twisted a little, then pulled it out. Lucky for me the bullet kept going rather than lodging in my flesh."

I tried to imagine pain like that, and the only thing I could remember was shooting my little toe off with Pa's rifle. Of course, I passed out right away then and didn't remember anything until I woke up at Doc's place with my foot wrapped tight.

We walked for a while more without speaking. The

only sound was the crunch of our boots in the snow. The moon was a sliver of light hanging over us, and I thought it was the most beautiful night I had ever seen in all my twelve years.

I wondered if when I grew up there would be a war for me to come home from like this, walking next to Pa, stride for stride with him.

HOMECOMING

FROM A HALF MILE AWAY we could see the orange light shining through the front window of our cabin. Davey stopped in the middle of the road. Pa and I turned around to look at him, wondering what was wrong.

"It sure looks peaceful," he said. "I dreamed a hundred times of walking over the hill like this and seeing home again. I'm afraid it is a dream and I'll wake up still in a trench."

"You think you're dreaming?" I said.

"I could be."

I knew one surefire way of proving he wasn't. I reached into the snowbank and molded a fine-looking ball, then threw it at Davey. It struck him right in the stomach.

"Hey!" he shouted at me. "What are you doing?"

"If it was a dream you wouldn't feel it, right?"

"You little . . ."

I took off running before he finished his sentence and made it to our cabin ahead of him. I put my hand on the handle, but the door opened out on me so fast I fell on my backside.

"I thought I heard commotion out here," Sadie said.

"It's Davey," I said. "He's back, Sadie, he's back."

She lifted me up and hugged me close to her. "And you're back, too, Jeremy."

"Oh, yeah, I forgot. I'm back, too."

Suddenly she pushed me away, then leaned forward and sniffed me, like Bite does to things sometimes. "What's that smell on you?"

"Do I smell sweet, Sadie?"

She sniffed again. "You smell like . . . like rum."

Pa and Davey came up just then. Davey dropped his bag on the ground and stuck out his hand to Sadie.

"I'm pleased you've come to live with us," he said.

Sadie brushed away his hand. "Oh, now, you're not too big for a hug, too." She wrapped her arms around him for a long time. When she pulled away she said, "You have your pa's size, I'd say."

"Almost," Davey said. "Maybe in another year."

"Let's get inside now," Pa said. "We've had a long day that none of us will ever forget."

Sadie shooed us in the door and brought out coffee and cheese biscuits. "Now," she said, "tell me everything."

Before I could open my mouth to tell her even a little *something*, Sadie came up sniffing the back of my neck. "What *is* that smell?" she said. "You take this boy to a drinking establishment, James Chance?"

"I did no such thing," Pa said. "And I'd think a woman such as yourself would know what he's smelling of."

"A woman such as myself?"

"Any woman who knows her way around the kitchen," Pa said.

Sadie leaned over me. Then she stuck her hand in my hair and pulled away. She smelled her fingers. "It's something familiar," she said, "but I can't place it"

"It's molasses!" I shouted. "I swam in molasses today, Sadie."

She looked at Pa to see if I was lying.

"That's about the truth of it," he said. "Jeremy swam in molasses today."

"Molasses? Well, I figure if ever a boy was born who could figure out a way to do that, you'd be the one."

"I didn't choose to, Sadie. A huge tank of molasses exploded all over everybody, not just me."

"Maybe that's so, but I can't help thinking that tank was just waiting until you got there to blow open."

As we ate our fill of cheese biscuits, I explained the molasses explosion to Sadie, and she kept saying things like, "Molasses? Thirty feet of molasses?" and, "People died from it?" and, "You're not trying to fool me now, are you?"

No matter what I said she was still not believing till Davey chimed in that he heard the explosion himself. Then Pa described what he saw. "Molasses everywhere," he said. "That city's going to smell sweet for years to come." He pushed his chair back from the table. "Time to bed now," he said. "We have to get up early tomorrow, get a jump on the day."

Davey and I looked at each other and couldn't help but laugh. "It's hard to believe," he said, "I missed hearing you say that, Pa."

We all stood up, but Sadie latched onto my arm. "This boy's going nowhere near his bed till the molasses has been scrubbed out of him."

"Ah, Sadie," I said, "I can't take a bath now."

"You can and you will," she said. "I won't have you getting molasses all over the sheets. James, bring out the tub and heat up some water."

Pa didn't look pleased at being ordered about, but he fetched the tub from the back and set it in the middle of the kitchen. Davey pumped water into a bucket and dumped it in the tub while Sadie heated up some on the stove. In a few minutes the bath was ready.

"Get out of those sticky things and into the water," she said.

I looked around. Pa was standing there, and Davey, and Sadie. She couldn't be expecting me to shuck my clothes in front of everybody. A boy who has run off to the city and been a hero shouldn't have to do that.

"What's holding you up?" Sadie asked.

Pa stepped up next to me. "A man needs some privacy taking a bath," he said.

Sadie looked at me. "A *man?*"

"That's what I called him," Pa said. "A *young* man, but still, a man. We'll go upstairs and let Jeremy see to himself."

"Mind you dunk your head," Sadie said. "And don't splash on the floor."

"He knows how to take a bath," Pa said as he coaxed her up the steps.

"Don't forget to wash behind your ears," Davey said, "and use the horse brush on your hair, and . . ."

I stuck my hand in the water and flicked some toward him. Pa turned just at that moment, and wouldn't you know the water hit him smack in the face.

I figured I was a goner, because Pa doesn't like fooling at all, much less inside the house. But then Sadie laughed and Davey laughed, and I vow I saw a smile coming on Pa before he wiped it away with his arm.

"The house has come alive again," Sadie said, "just as I told you."

———

I soaked in the warm water so long it turned almost to freezing. I didn't care. I'd never been left alone downstairs like this at night. The lamp on the table wasn't powerful enough to light up the corners of the cabin, but I wasn't afraid. Besides, Bite was nearby. He was dead asleep already, but I knew he'd wake up barking if anything tried to come through the door.

I had a lot of time to think as I scrubbed myself, and what I thought about was Pa. I'd worried all the way back to Derry that he'd tell Davey and Sadie about the rum balls and me being a thief. But he didn't say a word about it. I appreciated that. It was bad enough that *he* knew I stole, let alone Davey and Sadie, too.

I wondered if the Derry paper would carry news of the explosion in Boston, and would I be mentioned? I imagined the headline: "Runaway Boy Steals Rum Balls—God Sends Molasses Flood to Teach Him a Lesson." Pa said that's not the way it happened, and I guess he's right. The Lord wouldn't be exploding the molasses tank over a whole street just as a message to me. Besides, he has more important people on his mind to deal with.

But I did learn a lesson from my adventure: I was grown up in Pa's eyes, and getting in trouble couldn't be erased with a whipping anymore. Whatever I did now, bad or good, would stick to me as long as the molasses to the seat of my pants.

APOLOGY

NEXT DAY I WOKE with the first of the sun bursting through my window. I peeled my spruce gum off my bedpost and commenced to softening it up with my tongue. Then I turned to look outside to see what kind of day it was, and I was amazed at the sight. I had to rub my eyes to make sure what I was seeing. The spite fence was all knocked down around the black walnut in front of Cutter's place. It was just a bunch of wood lying in the snow.

"You're out of bed early."

I whirled, and there was Pa standing the doorway.

"Yes sir. Is Davey up?"

"You let him sleep in a while," Pa said. "This was his first night in a proper bed in a year."

I looked back outside, toward Cutter's. "You took the fence down, Pa."

Normally he didn't like me pointing out what was plain to see. He said that was a waste of breath. But this time he didn't admonish me.

"Chopped it down yesterday," he said, "before I went

after you. And this morning I'm going to haul the wood back to the barn."

I started pulling on my leggins over my union suit. "I'll help you."

"No, this is my work. I put the fool thing up, it's for me to take it down."

I slipped my suspenders over my shoulders. "What changed your mind about the fence, Pa?"

He twisted one end of his mustache. "You did."

"I did?"

"You ran away and opened my eyes. I'd forgotten what was important to me. It's you boys, not a tree."

I looked out of the window, and there was the black walnut, like it had been for all my years living. Sometimes when I woke in the night and the moon was low in the sky, that tree seemed like some giant crawling thing creeping across the field toward our house. It frighted me when I was little, and I used to run down the hall and jump in bed with Davey. It's funny what frights you, when you don't know better.

"It is a grand tree, Pa, especially in the spring."

"That it is. But I was looking at it and seeing furniture. I missed remembering that it's a tree, and one that means something special to someone."

"You know about Cutter and his wife?"

Pa nodded. "I went over to his place yesterday looking for you, and we talked things out. I thought about how I'd feel if someone wanted to cut down the maple that shades your ma's resting place on the hill. It made me ashamed that I'd done something so hateful to another man." Pa pulled me to him and gave me the hardest hug I could remember. He smelled like shaving cream. "As I was coming after you, Jeremy, I kept thinking what you said to me— that I was wrong."

I pulled away from him. "I'm sorry, Pa. I shouldn't have said that."

"No, boy, I'm apologizing to you for whipping you just because you spoke your mind. I already apologized to Cutter for the fence, and he forgave me for being so bull-headed. I'm asking you to do the same for the whipping."

It was hard at twelve years old to be the forgiver, because I wasn't sure I wanted to give up the Pa who was always right, even when he was wrong. It was a lot simpler accepting everything he said and did as gospel, even if it meant getting my hide tanned now and then. But those days were gone.

"I do, Pa. Forgive you, I mean."

He put his hands on my shoulders. "Thank you, Jeremy."

I couldn't believe what had come of this new year: my pa apologizing to me and to old man Cutter, too. It seemed to me that now The War was really over.

AFTERWORD

THE WORLD INHABITED in 1919 by young people like Jeremy Chance was undergoing dramatic change. Automobiles—primarily Model Ts—were becoming common sights on the roads, even in rural areas like Derry, New Hampshire. Some people still preferred four-legged transportation, though, and called out to passing drivers, "Get a horse!" In the sky overhead small airplanes soared like giant birds. Until people saw one for themselves, they often didn't believe the news that Orville and Wilbur Wright had in 1903 invented the flying machine.

World War I had just ended in Europe, where two million American soldiers sailed to help the British, French, and Russians defeat the German and Austrian armies. The Armistice ending the fighting was signed on November 11, 1918, at eleven o'clock in the evening—the eleventh hour of the eleventh day of the eleventh month. The United States commemorates this event on Veterans Day, when all American soldiers are remembered.

Almost ten million soldiers died in World War I, which people at the time thought of as "the war to end all wars." But fighting in the trenches of France or Germany was only one of the great dangers of the time. The other killer of the day attacked both soldiers and civilians alike. It was the Spanish Influenza, and, in this novel, it takes the life of Jeremy's mother.

The disease started with sneezes and coughs, then progressed to stomach aches, muscle soreness, and high temperatures. Doctors were baffled. Some thought a poisonous plant was the cause, while others suggested wearing too many clothes could bring on the disease. Many people became fearful of going outside, leaving churches, stores, and businesses half empty.

Whether by coincidence or not, the Spanish Influenza subsided about the same time the Great War ended. More than twenty million people worldwide died from the disease, double the casualties from combat. It wasn't until the 1930s that scientists determined the cause: a virus so tiny that thirty million of them could sit on the head of a pin. Doctors still don't know why this particularly deadly strain of influenza so suddenly appeared and just as suddenly disappeared.

By 1919 homes in large cities such as Boston had bathrooms, gas lighting, radios, and running water. There were stores nearby to buy bread, milk, meat, and clothes. But in the countryside, families lived quite differently. They raised much of their own food and made most of their clothes. Without television, computers, or telephones, families entertained each other at night, often by reading or telling stories.

For a boy growing up in Derry, Boston would have seemed an exotic place, about as far away as a trip to the North Pole today. Hoboes often "rode the rails" by hopping onto trains as they pulled out of stations. Runaway youngsters did the same, and sometimes they met up with more adventure than they expected.

Jeremy Chance walked right into the Great Molasses Flood that struck Boston's North End at half past noon on January 15, 1919. The United States was just about to enter the age of Prohibition, which barred the drinking of alcohol, with the passing of the Eighteenth Amendment to the Constitution. Inside the giant tanks of the old Purity Distilling on Commercial Street were more than two million gallons of molasses, from which rum was made.

Perhaps the tank was overfilled. Perhaps the sudden warmth on this winter day contributed to a disastrous fermentation of the molasses. All that is known for sure is that the rivets on the tank popped like gunfire, spilling the contents down Commercial Street. Frightened people thought that the plant had been bombed.

There is an old saying that goes, "You move slower than molasses in January." But these waves of molasses fifteen to thirty feet high rolled through Boston at about thirty-five miles an hour! The sticky, hot, brown liquid bowled over people and moved buildings. The final death toll was twenty-one people, and dozens of horses were smothered in their stalls. In the novel, Jeremy was fortunate to be wearing several layers of clothes, which prevented his skin from being burned.

Even fifty years later—on certain hot, humid days—folks living in the North End said they could still smell the faint sweetness of molasses.

GEORGE HARRAR is the author of *Parents Wanted*, a novel about a young adopted boy who learns to love his new parents. He also wrote *Not As Crazy As I Seem*, in which a teenage boy copes with his obsessive-compulsive tendencies. His short fiction has appeared in numerous magazines for children and adults. His short story "The 5:22" won *Story* magazine's Carson McCullers Prize and was selected for the 1999 edition of *The Best American Short Stories*.

Harrar grew up in Jenkintown, Pennsylvania, and now lives in Wayland, Massachusetts, with his wife, Linda, a documentary filmmaker. They have one son, Tony.

The author's website is www.writer.georgeharrar.com.

IF YOU ENJOYED THIS BOOK, YOU'LL ALSO WANT TO READ THESE OTHER MILKWEED NOVELS.

To order books or for more information, contact Milkweed at (800) 520-6455 or visit our website (www.milkweed.org).

THE $66 SUMMER
by John Armistead

MILKWEED PRIZE FOR CHILDREN'S LITERATURE
NEW YORK PUBLIC LIBRARY BEST BOOKS OF THE YEAR: "BOOKS FOR THE TEEN AGE"

By working at his grandmother's general store in Obadiah, Alabama, during the summer of 1955, George Harrington figures he can save enough money to buy the motorcycle he wants, a Harley-Davidson. Spending his off-hours with two friends, Esther Garrison, fourteen, and Esther's younger brother, Bennett, the unusual trio in 1950s Alabama—George is white and Esther and Bennett are black—embark on a summer of adventure that turns serious when they begin to uncover the truth about the racism in their midst.

THE RETURN OF GABRIEL
by John Armistead

When Cooper Grant, Jubal Harris, and Squirrel Kogan form a secret society called the Scorpions, they set their sights on getting even with the school bully, Reno McCarthy. But it's 1964, and as civil rights workers descend on their small Mississippi town and the KKK gathers to respond, tension begins to rise. The boy's camaraderie and courage are tested as each is swept up into the tumultuous events of "Freedom Summer."

GILDAEN: THE HEROIC ADVENTURES OF A MOST UNUSUAL RABBIT
by Emilie Buchwald
CHICAGO TRIBUNE BOOK FESTIVAL AWARD, BEST BOOK FOR AGES 9–12

Gildaen is befriended by a mysterious being who has lost his memory but not the ability to change shape at will. Together they accept the perilous task of thwarting the evil sorcerer, Grimald, in this tale of magic, villainy, and heroism.

THE OCEAN WITHIN
by V. M. Caldwell
MILKWEED PRIZE FOR CHILDREN'S LITERATURE

Elizabeth is a foster child who has just been placed with the boisterous and affectionate Sheridans, a family that wants to adopt her. Accustomed to having to fend for herself, however, Elizabeth is reluctant to open up to them. During a summer spent by the ocean with the eight Sheridan children and their grandmother, dubbed by Elizabeth as "Iron Woman" because of her strict discipline, Elizabeth learns what it means—and how much she must risk—to become a permanent member of a loving family.

TIDES
by V. M. Caldwell

Recently adopted twelve-year-old Elizabeth Sheridan is looking forward to spending the summer at Grandma's oceanside home. But on her stay there, she faces problems involving her cousins, five-year-old Petey and eighteen-year-old Adam, that cause her to question whether the family will hold together. As she and Grandma help each other through troubling times, Elizabeth comes to see that she has become an important member of the family.

ALLIGATOR CROSSING
by Marjory Stoneman Douglas

Near the strange wilderness that forms Everglades National Park, young Henry Bunks has made a secret hideaway for himself to which he can flee from the teasing and bullying of his older schoolmates. In this tense and colorful story, the hideaway becomes the starting place for a string of adventures involving an outlaw alligator hunter, a roving botanist, a girl traveling with her father in a palatial cruiser, and, above all, the vast Everglades. Setting and story are tautly linked as Henry finds himself serving the alligator hunter first as unwilling accomplice and finally as rescuer.

PARENTS WANTED
by George Harrar
MILKWEED PRIZE FOR CHILDREN'S LITERATURE

After five "adoption parties" and no luck, Andy Fleck, the kid nobody wanted, faces his biggest challenge yet—learning how to live with parents who seem to love him. Placed in an adoptive home with Jeff and Laurie, he has a chance to get out of the grip of his past, which includes a jailed father and a mother who gave him up to the state. But Andy can't keep himself from challenging every limit that his adoptive parents set. So far, Laurie and Jeff have refused to give up on their difficult new son. But will he go too far?

No Place
by Kay Haugaard

Arturo Morales and his fellow sixth-grade classmates decide to improve their neighborhood and their lives by building a park in their otherwise concrete, inner-city Los Angeles barrio. The kids are challenged by their teachers to figure out what it would take to transform the neighborhood junkyard into a clean, safe place for children to play. Despite their parents' skepticism and the threat of street gangs, Arturo and his classmates struggle to prove that the actions of individuals—even kids—can make a difference.

The Monkey Thief
by Aileen Kilgore Henderson
NEW YORK PUBLIC LIBRARY BEST BOOKS OF THE YEAR: "BOOKS FOR THE TEEN AGE"

Twelve-year-old Steve Hanson is sent to Costa Rica for eight months to live with his uncle. There he discovers a world completely unlike anything he can see from the cushions of his couch back home, a world filled with giant trees and insects, mysterious sounds, and the constant companionship of monkeys swinging in the branches overhead. When Steve hatches a plan to capture a monkey for himself, his quest for a pet leads him into dangerous territory. It takes all of Steve's survival skills—and the help of his new friends—to get him out of trouble.

THE SUMMER OF THE BONEPILE MONSTER
by Aileen Kilgore Henderson
MILKWEED PRIZE FOR CHILDREN'S LITERATURE
ALABAMA LIBRARY ASSOCIATION 1996 JUVENILE/YOUNG ADULT AWARD
MAUDE HART LOVELACE AWARD FINALIST

Eleven-year-old Hollis Orr has been sent to spend the summer
with Grancy, his father's grandmother, in rural Dolliver, Alabama,
while his parents "work things out." As summer begins, Hollis
encounters a road called Bonepile Hollow, barred by a gate and
a real skull and crossbones mounted on a board. "Things that go
down that road don't ever come back," he is told. Thus begins
the mystery that plunges Hollis into real danger.

TREASURE OF PANTHER PEAK
by Aileen Kilgore Henderson
NEW YORK PUBLIC LIBRARY BEST BOOKS OF THE YEAR: "BOOKS FOR THE TEEN AGE"

Twelve-year-old Page Williams begrudgingly accompanies her
mother, Ellie, as she flees her abusive husband, Page's father. Together they settle in a fantastic new world—Big Bend National
Park, Texas. Wild animals stalk through the park, and the nearby
Ghost Mountains are filled with legends of lost treasures. As
Page tests her limits by sneaking into forbidden canyons, Ellie
struggles to win the trust of other parents. Only through their
newfound courage are they able to discover a treasure beyond
what they could have imagined.

I AM LAVINA CUMMING
by Susan Lowell
MOUNTAINS & PLAINS BOOKSELLERS ASSOCIATION AWARD

In 1905, ten-year-old Lavina is sent from her home on the Bosque
Ranch in Arizona Territory to live with her aunt in the city of
Santa Cruz, California. Armed with the Cumming family motto,

"courage," Lavina deals with a new school, homesickness, a very spoiled cousin, an earthquake, and a big decision about her future.

THE BOY WITH PAPER WINGS
by Susan Lowell

Confined to bed with a viral fever, eleven-year-old Paul sails a paper airplane into his closet and propels himself into mysterious and dangerous realms in this exciting and fantastical adventure. Paul finds himself trapped in the military diorama on his closet floor, out to stop the evil commander, KRON. Armed only with paper and the knowledge of how to fold it, Paul uses his imagination and courage to find his way out of dilemmas and disasters.

THE SECRET OF THE RUBY RING
by Yvonne MacGrory
WINNER OF IRELAND'S BISTO "BOOK OF THE YEAR" AWARD

Lucy gets a very special birthday present—a star ruby ring— from her grandmother and finds herself transported to Langley Castle in the Ireland of 1885. At first, she is intrigued by castle life, in which she is the lowliest servant, until she loses the ruby ring and her only way home.

EMMA AND THE RUBY RING
by Yvonne MacGrory

Only one day short of her eleventh birthday and looking forward to spending time with her dad, Emma wakes up not at her cousin Lucy's, where she has been visiting, but in a nineteenth-century Irish workhouse. Emma learns that the ruby ring can grant two wishes to its wearer, and now, at a time of dire historical unrest, she must prove she can be the heroic girl she wants to be.

A Bride for Anna's Papa
by Isabel R. Marvin
MILKWEED PRIZE FOR CHILDREN'S LITERATURE

Life on Minnesota's iron range in 1907 is not easy for thirteen-year-old Anna Kallio. Her mother's death has left Anna to take care of the house, her young brother, and her father, a blacksmith in the dangerous iron mines. So she and her brother plot to find their father a new wife, even attempting to arrange a match with one of the "mail order" brides arriving from Finland.

Minnie
by Annie M. G. Schmidt
WINNER OF THE NETHERLANDS' SILVER PENCIL PRIZE AS ONE OF THE BEST BOOKS OF THE YEAR

Miss Minnie is a cat. Or rather, she *was* a cat. She is now a human, and she's not at all happy to be one. As Minnie tries to find and reverse the cause of her transformation, she brings her reporter friend, Mr. Tibbs, news from the cats' gossip hotline—including revealing information that one of the town's most prominent citizens is not the animal lover he appears to be.

The Dog with Golden Eyes
by Frances Wilbur
MILKWEED PRIZE FOR CHILDREN'S LITERATURE
TEXAS LONE STAR READING LIST

Many girls dream of owning a dog of their own, but Cassie's wish for one takes an unexpected turn in this contemporary tale of friendship and growing up. Thirteen-year-old Cassie is lonely, bored, and feeling friendless when a large, beautiful dog appears one day in her suburban backyard. Cassie wants to adopt the dog, but as she learns more about him, she realizes that she is, in fact, caring for a full-grown Arctic wolf. As she attempts to protect the wolf from urban dangers, Cassie discovers that she possesses strengths and resources she never imagined.

BEHIND THE BEDROOM WALL
by Laura E. Williams

MILKWEED PRIZE FOR CHILDREN'S LITERATURE
NEW YORK PUBLIC LIBRARY BEST BOOKS OF THE YEAR: "BOOKS FOR THE TEEN AGE"
MAUDE HART LOVELACE AWARD FINALIST
SUNSHINE STATE YOUNG READER'S AWARD MASTER LIST
JANE ADDAMS PEACE AWARD HONOR BOOK

It is 1942. Thirteen-year-old Korinna Rehme is an active member of her local *Jungmädel*, a Nazi youth group, along with many of her friends. Korinna's parents, however, secretly are members of an underground group providing a means of escape to the Jews of their city and are, in fact, hiding a refugee family behind the wall of Korinna's bedroom. As Korinna comes to know the family, especially their young daughter, her sympathies begin to turn. But when someone tips off the Gestapo, loyalties are put to the test and Korinna must decide in what she believes and whom she trusts.

THE SPIDER'S WEB
by Laura E. Williams

Thirteen-year-old Lexi Jordan has just joined "the Pack," a group of neo-Nazi skinheads, as a substitute for the close-knit family she wishes she had. After she and the Pack spray paint a synagogue, Lexi hides from her pursuers on the front porch of elderly Ursula Zeidler's home, a former member of the Hitler Youth Group, who painfully recalls her ugly anti-Semitic Nazi activities and betrayal of a friend. When her younger sister becomes enthralled with Lexi's new "family," Lexi realizes the true meaning of the Pack and has little time to save herself and her sister from its sinister grip.

Join Us

Since its genesis as *Milkweed Chronicle* in 1979, Milkweed has helped hundreds of emerging writers reach their readers. Thanks to the generosity of foundations and of individuals like you, Milkweed Editions is able to continue its nonprofit mission of publishing books chosen on the basis of literary merit—the effect they have on the human heart and spirit—rather than on the basis of how they impact the bottom line. That's a miracle our readers have made possible.

In addition to purchasing Milkweed books, you can join the growing community of Milkweed supporters. Individual contributions of any amount are both meaningful and welcome. Contact us for a Milkweed catalog or log on to www.milkweed.org and click on "About Milkweed," then "Supporting Milkweed," to find out about our donor program, or simply call (800) 520-6455 and ask about becoming one of Milkweed's contributors. As a nonprofit press, Milkweed belongs to you, the community. Milkweed's board, its staff, and especially the authors whose careers you help launch thank you for reading our books and supporting our mission in any way you can.

Interior design by Christian Fünfhausen.
Typeset in 10/15 point Century
by Stanton Publication Services.
Printed on acid-free 50# Fraser Trade Book paper
by Friesen Corporation.